Suzy
Who?

Suzy Who?

WINIFRED MADISON

SCHOLASTIC BOOK SERVICES
New York Toronto London Auckland Sydney Tokyo

ISBN: 0-590-31822-5

Copyright © 1979 by Winifred Madison. All rights reserved. Published by Scholastic Book Services, a division of Scholastic Magazines, Inc.

15 14 13 12 11 10 9 8 7 6 5 4 3   0 1 2 3 4 5/8

Chapter 1

On a sprightly September morning just before she would go to high school for the first time, Suzy Simmons gazed at herself in the mirror over the bureau in her bedroom. She may have been praying. Or possibly she was stating a long list of wishes, demands, and pleas to anyone who might be listening. Alpha VII, a bright yellow parakeet as noisy as the six birds who had preceded him and been murdered by Marmaduke the cat, perched on Suzy's shoulder and babbled parakeet wisdom in her ear. Possibly he was agreeing with everything she said.

"Please, let this year be IT. Something different. Junior high was so awful. I'm so tired of being nothing. Now I want to be SOMEBODY. Have lots of friends, new friends who will like me. I want to go to parties, dances, games. Well, at least one party, one dance, one game . . . And" — an involuntary nervous giggle escaped her — "I'd like to fall in love. You know, just out of curiosity. Just to see what it's like."

She could have continued this list for at least ten

1

minutes more. After two years in which she had sailed through junior high, practically unknown, that is not once having been asked to a party or a dance or even to join the crowd at Fountain Blue for a milkshake, she had had time enough to compile at least five pages of wishes.

But at the moment she was interrupted by an angry racket going on downstairs, and although she guessed quite accurately what was probably happening, still she was compelled to go down and see.

It was an old familiar argument. Her father, her mother, and her small sister, Cynthia, stood around the indoor garden that had been artfully if inconveniently placed between the hall and the living room. Dr. Simmons, glowering, held a huge marmalade colored tomcat in his arms, grasping the paws firmly to avoid being clawed to death.

"Evelyn," he was saying to his wife, "Damcat has to go. This is the third Bird of Paradise he's scratched around, and you know the other two died, and this probably will too. He's costing us a fortune in plants, to say nothing of the mess. He's got to go."

Dr. Simmons, ordinarily a mild man, was not swearing. Damcat was his name for Cynthia's cat. Cynthia took Marmaduke into her arms and held him close to her tiny bosom. He was an enormous cat with patches of fur nicked here and there where he had engaged in fights, but now he leered at Dr. Simmons with a smug "so there!" as he felt himself safe in Cynthia's arms.

A garden inside the house was the idea of the decorator who convinced Mrs. Simmons that an atrium was as chic as anyone could get in Elmwood

Heights. Dr. Simmons had foreseen difficulties such as this, but Mrs. Simmons could not resist the tropical ferns and exotic (costly) plants that gave them status.

"Evelyn, something's got to go. This garden or that cat. There's a shelter for cats like that."

"No!" Cynthia cried, bearing Marmaduke to the kitchen where she poured him a saucer of half and half and fed him her father's unfinished bacon.

"Oh dear," said Mrs. Simmons weakly. "After all, it is Cynthia's pet. I would hate to hurt her feelings, stunt her emotional growth."

"You can't stunt Cynthia," Suzy remarked. "I think we should give that killer to the shelter and pick up a sweet little puppy instead. I'd train him, honest, I would."

Mrs. Simmons' voice became more definitive. "One animal in the house is enough."

"Besides," Dr. Simmons added regretfully, "that cat could make hamburger out of an Irish wolfhound, never mind an innocent puppy. Sorry, Pumpkin."

He patted Suzy on the shoulder and disappeared into the studio (made-over garage) to put the finishing touches on a piece of sculpture before leaving for his office. Mrs. Simmons bustled about the kitchen, watering hanging baskets of ferns and spider plants which the decorator had thrust on her and which she dared not abandon, even though she had to get up half an hour earlier than she liked so that she could finish watering them and get to her real estate office in time.

Practically alone now, Suzy placed herself before the hall mirror and continued with her pleas.

"A dog. Almost more than anything else, I want

a dog to be MY dog. A dog to run with me, to romp in the yard, to sleep at the foot of my bed.

"And I want long hair. Just once in my life, I want real long hair.

"And about those new friends. . . ." She saw herself in the center of a dozen vibrant, laughing friends, both male and female, as alive and enviable as a Pepsi party on a TV commercial. "Not that I don't like Patty and Mousie or anything like that, but they drag. Do you know what I mean?"

She could not explain her precise feelings further because the door chimes rang, sounding *Tea for Two*, her mother's idea.

"Oh shoot," Suzy said. She had wanted to walk into high school alone, particularly on this first day, and she feared that Patty would be waiting for her, just as if they were still going to junior high. Suzy winged around the indoor garden, barely escaping the clutches of a new cut leaf philodendron that had been planted there the week before to replace a rare bamboo dug up by Marmaduke. She opened the door and, of course, there was Patty, round face scrubbed pink and clean, yellow hair newly washed and brushed, and eyes shining as if she, too, had hopes like Suzy.

"Hi, Patty," Suzy said weakly. "You look nice."

That was true, for a warm, pleasant, kitcheny, basket-of-muffins look clung about Patty, but oh, she was fat, fat, really fat. Suzy cringed when mean people referred to her as Fatty Patty, something she would never do. Besides Suzy herself, though by no means fat, was rounded, too rounded to achieve those admirable high cheekbones she wished that she had.

"You ready?" Patty asked.

4

"Sure," Suzy said, grabbing her purse and a new notebook. Would it be junior high all over again, starting out the same old way? But she could not confess this to Patty or say she preferred to be alone.

"Good-bye," she called out to her father or mother, as if this were any ordinary day and not something special like the beginning of high school. A few muffled good-byes drifted from the kitchen, but no cheers, no huzzahs, no well-wishing kisses.

Suzy and Patty made their way through the flagstone path that snaked and twisted through an outdoor garden down to the sidewalk in a labyrinthine way that was supposed to suggest nature, the decorator said. The two girls had not gone half a block when they heard a faint nasal voice.

"Hey, you guys, wait for me!"

It was a mournful desperate voice, suggesting that the caller was being left behind on a rockbound desert island forever.

"It's Mousie. Let's wait for her," Patty said faithfully.

"Sure," Suzy agreed tonelessly.

Mousie, whose real name was Mary Lou, a fact which had long since been forgotten, took her time catching up with her friends. A Pitiful Pearl sort of girl, she could easily have been taken for an abandoned orphan with her thin body, long thin legs, and pale, pinched appearance that suggested she had never in all her life been fed or loved. Actually, Mousie lived in one of the largest and most impressive homes in Elmwood Heights, and if she died of malnutrition, it would not be because there was nothing to eat in the house but that she insisted it be fed to her spoonful by spoonful. As

5

she joined her friends, they murmured about her new clothes, new Ditto pants, a sleeveless sweater with hand-embroidered flowers, and a silk shirt from which the price tag dangled. As usual, her eyes were covered by fashionably dark glasses.

A constant complainer, she whined, "It's so far to the high school. Why don't we ride our bikes?"

"They get stolen there," Patty said, a good excuse for someone who found herself too fat to ride comfortably.

Suzy pulled the price tag from Mousie's shirt and the three of them walked on. "I think high school will be wonderful," Patty said dreamily. As usual, Mousie put her down.

"It will be as scummy as junior high. Just as boring. And more crowded. It's three times as big."

Suzy, walking between her fat friend and her thin friend, closed her eyes. Her first instinct was to rush ahead and leave them behind. It was a new life she wanted, not junior high all over again. But of course, she couldn't leave her friends for they were her only friends, if she didn't count Kate Osborne, who called her when she needed help with her math, which was at least two or three times a week.

She said almost nothing. As they approached the high school with its green lawns and wide open doors toward which hundreds of students were streaming, among which she recognized only a few from junior high, Suzy crossed her fingers, shut her eyes and silently made one last heartfelt request.

"Please, God, let something happen!"

Chapter 2

Somewhere, somehow, Suzy's prayers, demands, or pleas were heard, but they would not register for some time. There was nothing for Suzy to do but wait and trust.

The first day of school answered one heartfelt wish. High school was indeed different from junior high, somehow more grown-up, more exciting, more promising. But she felt more unknown than ever. Not even Suzy-What's-Her-Name, but simply one of many newcomers, a girl with a round face, short brown hair, and wide brown eyes.

After school Kate Osborne, her third friend (?), invited her over to her house for root beer, which, translated, meant she wanted Suzy to help her with math, the same now as when they were in junior high. Suzy hesitated.

"Honest, Suzy, math is so hard for me and my parents'll kill me if I don't get through it. I can't understand a word that Mr. Stone said this morning, and my parents keep saying. . ."

"All right," Suzy interrupted weakly, having

heard this story many times. "But just this once."

It was an ethical matter, for Suzy believed that one should help when asked. But something else weighed in the balance. Kate did have many friends and made promise after promise to Suzy to "get her in the clique." But she had not yet asked Suzy, not once. Possibly in high school, Kate would remember her promises and come through.

They drank root beer and nibbled taco chips while Suzy not only explained but practically did the math assignment. When that was over, Kate praised Suzy as usual. "You are SOOOO smart in math. If only I had one tenth of your brain. Say, what time is it? Whoops, I almost forgot. I have to meet my mother; we're getting new shoes. But you are a DOLL to help me and I'll never forget. Suzy, you're real neat and someday I'm going to do something nice for you. Wait and see!"

Suzy walked home discouraged. High school had not changed Kate one bit, at least not yet.

"Make new friends. That's what you have to do," Suzy's mother said after dinner as they both cleared away the dinner dishes and put the kitchen in order. Mrs. Simmons' advice was plentiful, blunt, free, and often sound, but Suzy felt honor-bound to reject it even when she agreed with her mother. Mrs. Simmons was mentioning the names of half a dozen "young people" she knew, children of her friends. If Suzy had any sense, she inferred, she'd seek them out.

"Yech," said Suzy, pretending to be sick. "Anyway, I have friends."

"With friends like Patty, Mousie, and Kate, you don't need enemies," Mrs. Simmons said, a remark Suzy particularly hated because it was such a cliché,

8

and she'd heard it so many times before. But Mrs. Simmons, oblivious to Suzy's feelings, went right on.

"Suzy, you have to take the first steps. Find one or two new friends; then that will lead to other friends, boyfriends, dates, parties, games, and all the things that young girls want. Then eventually there'll be college, even more fun, and after that. . ."

"Boy, you sure are worried I'm just going to be an old maid, aren't you?"

"Don't be silly. I don't think any such thing." Mrs. Simmons answered so quickly that it confirmed Suzy's own worries. It could be true, that she could possibly grow older and older, drying up, going through high school, college, and the rest of life without a single date, without ever having gone to a party, without ever having fallen in love.

"Anyway, I don't care. I DON'T CARE," Suzy shouted.

"All right then, you don't care, but you don't have to be so noisy about it, do you?" Mrs. Simmons said in a low, reasonable voice. She put her arm around Suzy and gave her a quick, affectionate hug before going on to scrub the sink, but she sighed, a tiny unmistakable sigh which Suzy interpreted as: "I give up. I've tried everything with that girl and now I give up."

At that point, Suzy was ready to give up on herself.

But on the third day of school, something happened. At first it appeared to be simply an accident, nothing more than an incident, a casual event. Still it would have repercussions in time.

Although Suzy still walked to school each day with Patty and Mousie, her classes differed from theirs, and so she was alone much of the day. Between third and fourth period she had to rush from English class at one end of the building to chemistry at the other, through corridors packed with students, some of whom horsed around almost as much as though this were still junior high. Yet it was more sophisticated horsing, she decided.

On that third day of school, four boys were walking down the hall, throwing a volleyball from one to another over the heads of the crowds, joking with one another all the way. Suzy would not have thought anything of this, in fact she would hardly have noticed it, had there not been an accident. A tall blond boy who jumped up and leaned backward to catch a particularly high ball bumped into Suzy. He threw her off balance so that she fell to the ground, books scattering everywhere and a pen rolling under the feet of someone who kicked it on so that it was lost forever.

Suzy sat up, tears in her eyes, not so much because her posterior hurt with the insult of the sudden jolt, but because she was so embarrassed. Immediately she pulled her jean skirt over her knees as the boy responsible for her fall kneeled beside her.

"I'm sorry. I'm really sorry. Nothing personal. It was an accident, pure accident. Are you hurt?"

The tears retreated and her mouth opened slowly. Never in all her life had Suzy met such a beautiful person. She had been told not to use the word "beautiful" to apply to a male, but there was no other word for this tall boy with straight silky hair so blond and long he had to shake his head to move it out of his eyes. The bluest of eyes looked into Suzy's with an expression of concern. Then he smiled encouragingly. His skin was transparent, almost luminous. His was the kind of beauty like that of a hero on a wide movie screen, or a painting of one of King Arthur's knights. All his clothes were white, gauze shirt, duck pants, white socks, white tennis shoes. A White Knight. All this she took in while he held out his hand to help her up.

"I'm all right. It's okay," Suzy whispered.

"Let me help you," he said, gathering her books since she didn't appear to need his help in getting up. His friends waited for him, joshing him mildly.

"That's it, Peter. Pick on the new kids. Knock 'em down every time."

"Hey, watch out for this guy. He's dangerous," another one of his friends called out.

"Don't listen to them. They're crazy," Peter said. "You're sure everything is okay, no bones broken?"

"Really, it's nothing. I didn't mind at all," Suzy answered, immediately aware that it sounded as though she were giving him permission to knock her down any time.

"See ya," he said, grinning as he disappeared in the crowd.

So that was Peter. Peter who? Somebody important, of that she was sure, but how would she find out? Kate Osborne would know for she knew who everybody was, but Suzy couldn't possibly ask her. It would be best to keep the incident to herself like a cherished secret. Not even Patty or Mousie would know.

After school Mousie invited Suzy and Patty swimming, for it was a warm day. While Mousie, who never swam at all, sat swathed in sweaters at the edge of an extravagantly long swimming pool

11

and Patty joined her, Suzy swam laps up and down. She was spinning her first fantasies about Peter.

They would most likely pass in the halls each day. He would smile at her at first, then say hello and one day, possibly the middle of the next week, he would approach her.

"I'm Peter," he would say modestly, "and I won't be able to sleep until I find out who you are."

"Suzy," she would answer, blushing a little. The pink cheeks were becoming.

"I think I ought to make up for knocking you down last week. Want to meet me at Fountain Blue after school?"

"I guess I can manage it for a little while," she would say hesitantly. Her mother had warned her that a girl should not be too eager.

Fountain Blue, the local ice cream store, was the gathering place for the high school crowd, the place to go. Suzy was inventing conversations between them, witty, sophisticated, and yet hardly concealing a growing warmth, a certain sweetness.

The next day as she walked from English class to chem, she was fairly certain that the increased thumping of her heart meant she was falling in love. This time Peter walked in a graceful, leisurely way, still wearing white clothes, while the crowds rushed around him. It was not until Suzy nearly passed him, that she saw the girl walking beside him and her mouth opened involuntarily in a surprised and possibly disappointed "oh." This girl was certainly Somebody. Ripples of long, curling, blond hair, eyes nearly as blue as his (or were they green? Impossible to tell in that quick encounter), a figure that was slender yet full—she appeared to have a certain magnetism almost as strong as Peter's. At least Suzy could not tear her eyes away from either of them. No wonder Peter did not even notice Suzy, let alone look for her and confess he couldn't sleep for thinking of her.

The daydreams and fantasies faded, useless now. Yet a painful and delicious curiosity replaced them. Who were these people, these superior beings?

Three days later she found out. At a school assembly in the auditorium the principal and half a dozen students, including Peter and the girl, sat on the stage. The principal spoke first and said how everyone must do their share to bring spirit to the school, or whatever it is that principals say to the student body when the season is new. Then he introduced the captain of the football team, a large, handsome L'il Abner hero named Al Sakovich, who mumbled words of encouragement about the team. He was followed by a pleasant girl representing the AFS, a string bean of a boy who talked about musical organizations, and a small, bright chipmunk of a boy who represented the Science Club. Suzy thought she would faint if Peter were not introduced soon.

"Do I really have to introduce this fella?" the principal asked. The crowd burst into cheers and Suzy bit her fingernail in frustration until the principal introduced him after all and the girl as well. "These are two of the most glamorous seniors in the school. Peter Gilbert and Melissa Schmerz. Shall we have a hand for them?"

Peter, dressed in still another white outfit, smiled broadly to the audience as if that smile were a secret message to each person there. He stepped forward,

13

placed an electric guitar around his neck, and quieted the crowd with an upraised hand.

"All right, all right, everyone! Let's have it all together. Everyone sing. How about that?"

He sang, and although the audience mumbled along after him, it was his voice that sang out over the crowd. Suzy held on to her seat, afraid she would faint with excitement although she had never before fainted in her life. Wonderful, wonderful Peter!

He signaled to the blond girl.

"C'mon, honey. C'mon, Melissa," he called and she stood beside him and now both of them sang, moving back and forth from side to side like singing stars on the Merv Griffin show. Schmerz was not a particularly happy name, Suzy decided, but with so radiant a personality, it didn't matter. She could get away with it. Suzy warned herself she must not become jealous, yet if she could snap her fingers and make Melissa vanish, she would not hesitate to do so.

The crowd roared. Finally Peter called for quiet as he made a pitch for the Dramatic Club. "This year we have terrific plans. Three fabulous one act plays this fall. And in the spring we are going to do a musical, a famous Broadway musical, but I can't tell you which one, not yet, only that it's the biggest and the best this school has ever done. We're gonna be wanting lots of support, actors, actresses, singers, dancers, people to do the lighting, the staging, the costumes . . . the whole thing."

"You tell 'em, Peter."

He couldn't go on for the cheers that followed. Why, Suzy thought, he has to be the most popular boy in the whole school. The principal announced

14

it was time to leave, but the whole school took up a cry.

"We want Peter! We want Peter! We want Peter!"

Peter, obviously loving this popularity, shrugged his shoulders helplessly and sang one more song, this time a popular sentimental song. "Are you a dream, or are you real? I cannot tell, my love. . ."

Suzy poured out of school with the rest of the crowd, hardly aware that Patty was begging her to go over to her house and taste some gingerbread she'd made the night before, or that Mousie complained that Suzy was changing. "You just don't listen anymore. You're in a fog."

"Uh-huh!" Suzy murmured. She wasn't walking along the streets of Elmwood Heights; she was floating. She had begged to fall in love ("Just to see what it was like, you know!"), and now she knew it was a delicious thing to do. She had indeed fallen (literally, at first) in love with Peter Gilbert. His blond image filled her mind.

Was he a dream or was he real?

As for Melissa Schmerz, Suzy let her fade and vanish, as if she didn't exist.

From now on, Suzy was thinking, everything will be different. It had already begun. Other dreams would come true, her life would change, and she, herself, would change. She could hardly wait for it all to happen.

Chapter 3

Sunday, being very Sunday-ish indeed, with heavy lowering skies and unexpected early rains, Suzy was about to lock herself up in her room when Mousie phoned, begging her to come and spend the afternoon with her.

"My parents have gone to some kind of a thing and I'm here all alone. Anyway, I want to read you my latest mystery novel. This has to be the most ingenious murder ever invented. You'll love it. I'll give you a hint: It's done with bubble gum."

Mousie wrote mystery novels, most of them gripping and fascinating, particularly if one liked a new corpse, ingeniously murdered, on every other page. As far as Suzy could tell, writing was Mousie's greatest virtue.

"I'd love to hear it, Mousie, but I gotta study. We have to memorize a poem in English. Another time. Okay?"

Mousie squeaked a bit and then hung up.

Suzy ran upstairs, shut the door of her room so that Alpha VII wouldn't fly out, and Marmaduke

(Killer) wouldn't come in after him. Then she threw herself across her bed where a fat English book lay waiting.

Suzy detested the bedspread, a ghastly lavender quilted covering that matched the quilting on the headboard. Almost everything in her room was chosen in violet shades, the purple rug, sprigs of lilac on the wallpaper, a desk covered with a harsh violet-blue plastic coating, and a decoration of Victorian pansies around the mirror. The decorator had assured Mrs. Simmons all young girls love lavender and she had told him to go ahead. But he had not known Suzy, who dreamed of a room that was white, or off-white, simple and pure.

Suzy opened her book, sighed, and immediately tried to find the shortest poem in the book. Approving the size, only eight lines and no title, of an Emily Dickinson poem, she began to read:

"I'm nobody! Who are you?
Are you nobody too?"

She closed the book, let her chin rest on her hand, and stared outside the window at the gray rain. The first lines of the poem could have been written for her.

"I'm nobody. That's right. Nobody. Suzy Who? Suzy Nobody."

She immediately made it clear to herself that she was not complaining or weeping with self-pity, something one would expect of Mousie, but was facing a fact objectively. A bit of truth there, Suzy Nobody. And the evidence? Her whole life provided that.

Even her mother would have agreed, not aloud of course, but privately. "Of course I love you," Mrs.

Simmons had said more than once. "After all, you're my daughter, aren't you?" But Suzy would have been happier if she had *liked* her as well, really liked her as she was. Mrs. Simmons was not so crude as to have said directly that she wished her daughter were a Bobbie Brown, who was a remarkable ballet dancer, or Francie Green, who won the Bank of America Awards for Good Citizenship every year, or Suzy's cousin, Julie, voted the most popular girl in high school. Fortunately this high school was in Massachusetts, 3,000 miles away, so that Suzy did not have to meet this paragon.

"You've had your chances," Mrs. Simmons said one night when she was particularly unhappy with Suzy. "You squandered them."

Suzy pondered this again and again. Her mother was right.

At the age of three, Suzy was sent to the most expensive nursery school in Elmwood Heights until she was expelled for climbing over the fence each morning and making mudpies with the infamous Jenkins kids who lived around the corner and took off *all* their clothes on hot days.

Ballet lessons at six. Suzy's right foot never knew what her left foot was doing. In the one recital where she appeared as a rosebud, a thread pulled. Unfortunately it was the thread which held the petals of her costume together, and so they fell off one by one, leaving Suzy a denuded rose (in pink panties) at the end of the dance. The teacher suggested that Suzy study tap dancing . . . elsewhere.

"Well, we can always try the violin," Dr. Simmons had said. After a year of scraping and scratching, the teacher, a passionate Yugoslavian concert violinist from Dubrovnik phoned Mrs. Simmons one day. "Meesus Seemons, you are vasting your time and money on Suzanne's lessons. The violin ees a delicate instrument. Perhaps another instrument, say the harmonica, would be more suitable."

And so it went. After three lessons on skis, Suzy broke both an arm and a leg. When they healed, she tried horseback riding but she insisted that the horses rolled their eyes and groaned whenever they saw her coming.

Even now Suzy appeared to fail in other ways too. Clothes. She insisted on jeans, shirts, and tee shirts. She compromised on a skirt made from old blue jeans, but if the Simmons family went out, a battle between Suzy and her mother was inevitable. The battle continued but somewhat in reverse as Mrs. Simmons and Marie, her hairdresser, insisted that Suzy's brown hair should be cut short and boyish; unexpectedly, Suzy craved long hair, but Mrs. Simmons always won.

Suzy was once invited to a party, although she hardly counted this as a bona fide invitation since her Aunt Gloria made her daughter, Jennifer, ask her cousin. Later Jennifer called when her mother wasn't around. "Hey, Suzy, you know this party I'm having on Saturday. Don't come. It's going to be terrible, all the kids you don't like. You can come if you want, but if I were you, I'd stay away."

And so she did. That marked the end of her professional and social life up to the present. A cipher.

In the first grades of school, Suzy judged her classmates on a simple YES, NO, and MAYBE classification system. The bright, pretty, and popular people were YES; the ugly, ignorant, or otherwise unacceptable classmates fell into the NO category; and MAYBE took in everyone who didn't fit anywhere else, including Suzy herself.

By the time Suzy reached the sixth grade, she changed her method of judging, using a one to ten rating. Patty and Mousie were barely three. Kate Osborne, who knew a number of people, achieved a six. Melissa Schmerz was such a positive ten, she may well have been a twelve (even on a one to ten rating), and Peter jumped the rating to a full fifteen, possibly a twenty.

As for herself, what was she? On the best of days a five minus, perhaps. On most days she was possibly a three. Thinking about it, she felt her rating getting lower and lower until she hovered somewhere between one and two.

Dreary Suzy Nobody! Were there no saving graces?

Actually, yes, for Suzy had a gift. It was not a great gift nor the one she would have chosen if she'd had anything to say about it, but there it was, like it or not. Mathematics. Most likely she was not nor would she become a genius, but she was undeniably good. At least, that is where she performed best, the field of numbers. And how did that happen? Lying on the bed, she thought of a possible explanation.

When she was a baby lying in her cradle, cooing and trying to fit all her toes in her mouth, the fairy godmothers stood around, scratched their heads, and asked one another what gifts they should give her.

"Can't give her brains," one said. "We already gave that to her big brother. Douglas the Brain, Princeton and all that."

"Can't give her beauty," the second one chimed in a high vinegary voice. "Gotta save that for the little sister who'll be coming along six years from now."

The third godmother peered into a sack of gifts and came up with a small, possibly secondhand gift, bruised at the edges but basically sound.

"A gift for numbers. For math. What about that?"

"It's small," the first one complained.

"But good enough for what's-her-name," the second one said.

They made the proper signs, mumbled the incantations, flew away for a martini celebration, and Suzy grew up counting fingers and toes in no time at all.

"But math really is terrific," Suzy was thinking. She had never been able to understand why Kate and so many others couldn't take to it. It was so beautifully logical. Unlike other subjects, there was no point whatever in making violent opinionated remarks about it. Two and two is four, no matter whether anyone approves it or not; it will never be three or five. That may be more certain than anything else in the world.

"And it's a challenge," she once stated at the dinner table. "Each problem says 'Go ahead, solve me. I dare you to do it!'" She had never been able to rest until she had mastered a problem. If only it were as easy to solve puzzles in life!

Mrs. Simmons was philosophical about Suzy's gift. "You can always be an accountant. It's a good enough living."

This statement horrified Suzy, for in her better

21

moments she had seen herself as a navigator in a spaceship, or a mathematician connected with the space program. Recalling this pleasant fantasy, Suzy changed her position, leaned back against the pillows with her hands behind her head.

Math is all right. Her teacher, Mr. Stone, sometimes referred to as Mr. Stoned or Mr. Stonehenge, was a bright-eyed man, terrifying at first, but he had obviously been pleased with Suzy.

"I could be the best in class," she thought, and that would make her a kind of somebody, although not a very important somebody. Still, she wasn't the best in class because of a rival, Daniel Bright, a boy no taller than she, whose brown eyes appeared to burn through the lenses of his glasses. When Mr. Stone asked for the solution to a problem, it was Daniel who shouted the answer at the same time that Suzy did. Yet he was a strange boy, so shy that he had never quite dared to glance at Suzy or anyone else.

And what did all this have to do with Peter? It meant that Suzy, in assessing her virtues, found few. There was nothing in her to admire, not the short ugly haircut (so different from Melissa's flowing locks) or any ability she might have. Most likely Peter Gilbert would not be impressed by a girl, a freshman at that, whose sole ability was math. It was hard to imagine him saying, "I just love the way you solved that geometry problem, Suzy." And there was nothing else to admire about her.

Once more the moody afternoon made her so heavy-hearted, she could not remember ever having felt so blue. Downstairs Cynthia and her friends — she had dozens of them — were banging out "Chopsticks" on the grand piano Dr. Simmons had bought for the new house even though nobody except Big Brother Brain could play it.

Suddenly restless, Suzy sprang from the bed, put on a raincoat, went outside, mounted her ten speed, and rode out of Elmwood Heights along a country road. The rain stopped and the sun appeared, barring the road with light and shade. The raindrops hanging from the tips of leaves sparkled, and soon she felt lighter. She could even imagine Peter riding beside her, curving around the bend with her, admiring the eucalyptus trees rustling above them, and stopping to watch as a deer crossed the road. It was so lovely, that he took her hand in his and neither of them could speak for a moment. Then he said:

"Suzy, I've never met anyone like you. You're so different. And it's so terrific to find you . . ." he said while the blue eyes sparkled.

The fantasies seemed to develop themselves, slipping easily from one to another. Without realizing it, Suzy had gone so far that when she turned around to go home, it was already getting dark. This meant a scolding, but it was worth it.

Soon Sunday would be over and Monday would come, and once more she would catch a glimpse of him as they passed each other in the hall.

Chapter 4

By the middle of October Suzy was discovering what being in love was like. "I hadn't expected it to be so uncomfortable," she admitted to herself. Being in love with someone who was barely aware of her existence became as tiresome as a prolonged game of tennis against a cement wall. Yet when she was about to give up the notion of Peter Gilbert and put him out of her mind forever, he would chance to see her in the hall or in the cafeteria and then he would dazzle her with a smile and a friendly "Hi!" as he passed her. And she began to dream of him again.

To be in love was a burden. His name kept rising to her lips. Sometimes she woke up in the middle of the night and found herself repeating his name, Peter Gilbert, Peter Gilbert. Visions of him appeared in her mind like a movie that had no end.

Math was the only release she had, for when she was confronted with a problem everything else in the world faded away and only Suzy and the problem were left. But she could hardly be expected to think of math all the time. On Saturdays she went to the public library to find the latest science fiction (a fine release there!) and frequently she bicycled out to the Animal Shelter at Woodknoll where Mr. Morales, the caretaker, gave her a leash and allowed her to exercise the animals in the large, fenced exercise area.

But the rest of the time Peter seemed to live within her. Now she knew why people in love walked around as if they were living on a different plane of existence. They were.

"Suzy, you're not listening to me at all. I can just tell," Patty complained one afternoon on the way home from school. "I was telling you how to make a Danish coffee cake. With yeast. I want you and Mousie to come and have some."

"Food is gross," Mousie said definitively and Suzy could see that poor Patty was beginning to feel let down by her friends.

"I adore coffee cake," Suzy said. "I'd love to have some."

(What am I doing? she thought. I shouldn't be eating all that sweet stuff, all that butter!) Yet she cajoled Mousie into going along with them and soon they were sitting in Patty's warm, cozy kitchen, drinking chocolate and tasting the most buttery of coffee cakes.

Yet while Patty talked, and while she answered and made herself appear interested, a movie reel was going on in her head, a fantasy in which she and Peter were at a high school dance. She was wearing a dress of soft, creamy, drifting stuff, possibly a warm shrimpy pink, while Peter, in formal

25

white, pressed his lips against her hair which was now a long, thick, curly brown mane. "My darling . . ." he murmured.

In a way it was safe to dream about Peter Gilbert because he was a star, so remote that nothing could possibly happen. He was like an actor whose face is spread out over a movie screen or a television set. She could not expect to become friendly any more than she could imagine herself going out with the Fonz or some of the rock stars she admired.

She almost wished he were already famous and somewhere else, for that would be easier than seeing him walk down the hall with his hand on the back of Melissa's neck as if he owned her and the two of them so concerned with each other that, except for an occasional glance at Suzy, they did not seem to know that she or anyone else existed. How hopeless it was, how discouraging!

Suzy desperately needed to talk to someone about Peter. But who?

Her mother? "A girl's mother is her best friend." Don't be ridiculous!

Then what about telling her friends? They knew something was different about Suzy. But it was too easy to predict what they would say.

Mousie would immediately become jealous. "You *would* find someone to fall in love with, but what about me? Nobody loves me. Nobody."

Then Suzy would have to reassure her. What a bore!

Patty's jaw would drop in surprise. "You in love? Ooo, what does your mother say?"

Really, sometimes Patty acted as if she were still ten years old.

However, Suzy was thinking, she could tell her father. He's special. Besides, he often confided in her, so possibly it would work the other way around. Sometimes friends ask, "Ugh, how does it feel to have a father who's a dentist?" Suzy had always considered this a ridiculous question, as if her father did nothing but drill her teeth or tell her to open wide, it isn't going to hurt, not very much.

Actually, at home Dr. Simmons ceased to be a dentist and became a sculptor, particularly on weekends. On a Sunday, Suzy slipped into his studio-garage filled with abstract sculptures, ranging from six inches to five feet in height — works in clay, plaster, and wood. On the far side of the garage, Dr. Simmons kept a massive block of wood which he occasionally hacked. But that afternoon Suzy found him working on a clay abstraction.

"Hi, Suzy, come in, pumpkin. I could use some company."

What he meant, Suzy suspected, was that he wanted her to admire his work. Wearing an old dentist's uniform, he added a piece of clay to the sculpture before him with a professional flourish.

"That's good, Dad. What is it?"

"An abstraction. I could call it 'Early Light' or 'Crisis' or some silly thing."

"Oh," Suzy said, "I'd like to see it all."

Dr. Simmons turned the piece on the turntable so that she could see it from every angle. Familiar forms she was certain he didn't intend emerged here and there, a molar, what appeared to be deep roots, and an unmistakable eyetooth jutting out from the clay. Should she tell him? It was very difficult to make the abstract forms Dr. Simmons loved, when dental parts automatically sneaked into the work.

"It's great, but did you intend to have a rotting molar there, Dad?"

"Where? Good heavens, you're right! I didn't see it until you mentioned it. Glad you told me," he said, although he did not appear glad.

"And this part down here looks like an open mouth with a tongue sticking out, at least from this angle," she said, and pointed out two other obvious teeth.

"Suzy," Dr. Simmons said, sitting on his stool. Dejected. "There's no escape. No matter how I try to get away from it, it keeps showing up."

"But, Dad, it's very strong. Really. You could exhibit it."

"H'm," he said mysteriously, the way he did when he had to tell a patient that a tooth must be extracted. He picked up a wooden tool and blocked out the offending tooth images in his work.

"How's everything going, Suzy?" he asked while taking off a gob of clay from one side of the piece and putting it on another.

"All right," she said. It wasn't easy to talk about Peter to a man who was smiling and then frowning at a big thing of clay.

"Is my favorite mathematician still leading the class?"

"In a way. I've got a rival. A boy."

"Are you holding your own?"

"Sure. But I'm not that competitive. The teacher's good and that's a big change."

She wanted to tell him about Peter. Maybe he would say forget it, and then she would, which would probably be wise. But of course, she didn't want to give up all this new daydreaming which made her life so rich. She approached the subject carefully.

"I was wondering, Dad. When you went to high school, did you have a girl friend? Or lots of them? Did you ever fall in love then?"

Another speculative h'm. "What did you say?" Dr. Simmons hadn't heard a word. His eyes were glazed on the sculpture and suddenly he brightened. "I've got it now, Suzy. No wonder it wasn't working. See, if I turn it upside down and put this mass of clay here so it balances that part that juts out there and the whole thing spirals upward. . . See what I mean? Suzy, you darling. If it weren't for your bright, sharp eyes, I'd never have gotten this thing underway."

"That's good," she said softly, giving up. There was no room there for confidences. Suzy kissed her father on the cheek, felt the brush of his mustache as he kissed her, and then she left.

Upstairs once more, she frowned. Someone had left the door of her room open. She had closed it. Cynthia's friends were in her room, playing.

"Alpha?" Suzy called her bird.

Usually Alpha, on hearing her name, flew down from wherever she might be perched to settle on Suzy's shoulder and chatter gossip in her ear. But she did not come.

"Alpha, come here! Alpha!" she called again, alarm in her voice.

Then she saw what she feared, a pitiful pile of yellow feathers and a small, crumpled body on the purple rug.

"Marmaduke! Killer cat! Killer! Murderer!"

She threw herself on the bed and sobbed, beating

against the headboard with her fists. That cat had killed seven birds, murdered the innocent lives, and nobody cared, nobody at all.

Then she saw Marmaduke swaggering along the hall. Proud of himself, he grinned up at her evilly.

"Killer!" she hissed at him. "Killer!"

Unable to stay in the house any longer, she picked up her library books and pedaled furiously to the library, a good place to go when it was impossible to stay home. She placed her books on the return shelf and went immediately, as usual, to the shelves where new books were displayed.

"Good luck at last!" A new Robert Heinlein was waiting to be grabbed. As she put her hand on it, it collided with the hand of someone else with the same impulse. Both hands withdrew immediately as if they had touched a hot wire. Then Suzy saw that it was Daniel Bright who apparently had the same idea, to get that new Heinlein.

"Go ahead. I guess you saw it first," Daniel said.

"No, that's all right. You can have it," she said.

"After you, Alphonse. I've got a pile already," he said, showing Suzy what he had already chosen, two books on advanced math, a detective story, and two science-fiction novels.

"Well, if you're sure you don't mind," Suzy said. "I can read it in two days or less and give it to you. But if you want it, that's okay."

"You take it. I didn't know you liked science fiction. Have you been into it very long?"

"In a way, I suppose. That's how I get off the planet," she said shyly. "And you?"

"I wouldn't put it like that. For me it's not exactly escape. There are too many possibilities talked about. They could come true, have come true in the past. When someone makes assumptions, I want to see if they hold up," Daniel explained and then, overcome by an unexpected reddening of his cheeks as if remembering his shyness, he mumbled, "See ya."

With that he rushed to get his books, checked out, and left.

"Interesting," Suzy thought, "but nothing like Peter. Not remotely." She began to wonder how Daniel would fit in her one to ten classification and stopped, baffled, unable to pin him down in the least. Thinking no more about it, except to grant that he had been quite decent about letting her take the Heinlein first, she found two more books, checked them out, and left.

The twilight air was changing from a faint violet to a deep blue, the time of day that Suzy loved. Then she remembered Alpha, poor little Alpha, and a sadness came over her again, but with it more understanding. It was asking too much of a cat not to go after a bird when this had been bred in him for thousands of years. Whoever had left the door open, possibly one of Cynthia's friends who didn't know it had to be closed. . .whatever. . .the "how" no longer mattered. Dr. Simmons would offer to buy her a parakeet, as he had before, but this time she would ask him not to do so. Seven tiny, feathered corpses were enough.

Mrs. Simmons said she was sorry, but it was Dr. Simmons who went to the garden to help Suzy bury Alpha the Seventh under a flowering plum.

The next day when Suzy returned from school, she found that the sad empty bird cage had been replaced by a handsome Boston fern. A card inside it read, "In memory of Alpha VII. With love, Mother."

Amazing! Suzy would have preferred a dog, but still this was a splendid surprise. She ran down to the kitchen and threw her arms around her mother.

"Thanks, Mom. That was a beautiful thing to do."

Life, she decided, unlike math, was frequently illogical. But that was quite all right.

Chapter 5

September, October, November, December, and now January. And in all that time nothing more happened where Peter was concerned, except that Suzy had developed volumes of fantasies. In her daydreams Melissa faded away, leaving Peter free, but at night Melissa had the distressing habit of appearing in Suzy's dreams, her green eyes flashing, just as Peter was about to kiss Suzy and tell her that he loved her. Suzy had also dreamed that during Christmas vacation Melissa would conveniently go away three thousand miles or so to visit her grandmother, Suzy would meet Peter unexpectedly somewhere, and since time was free, they would go for a long walk together and then. . .

But the holiday passed without a glimpse of Peter. Nothing interesting occurred, nothing at all, unless, of course, she counted some hairy games of chess that she played with Big Brother Brain, home from Princeton on Christmas vacation. Suzy felt sorry when he had to go back, and then the New

Year began and it was time to go back to school.

"Please," she prayed. "Let something happen! I can't go on like this. It's torture."

In a way her prayer was answered — a matter of interpretation. During that first week of school, a notice was passed around to each class:

OKLAHOMA, the musical comedy by Rodgers and Hammerstein, will be presented this spring. Tryouts for actors, actresses, dancers, and singers will be held on Wednesday after school in the auditorium.

Immediately Suzy knew she had to be in the play. Surely Peter would get the lead. Even the smallest part would mean being in his company.

"Oh, what a beautiful morning!" she sang to herself. Then the song faded, as she wondered how she would try out.

Dance? She would not dare.

Sing? That girl who from first grade on was invited to be a "listener" would never make it.

Act? The thought of being on a stage, confronting a sea full of beaming faces waiting for her to slip up on her lines or take a pratfall was more than she could imagine. Never would she let herself in for that, never.

If only she could choose her destiny, she would be born Melissa who could act, dance, sing, and be loved by Peter! But she was only Suzy, Suzy who knew all about two and two making four, as if that mattered!

Though she knew herself better than to try out for any part, still she went to the auditions and sat in back to watch the others. At least one hundred signed up for the 23 acting roles, and practically another hundred were intent on getting into the chorus or taking on the dancing roles. Mr. Rossetti, the director, wiped his brow and announced it might take a week to give everyone a chance.

The minor parts were given first, followed by the more important parts, leading up to Curley and Laurie. That anyone would dare to compete with Peter or Melissa was a sign of sheer madness, Suzy thought. And yet, even Suzy had to admit these courageous or foolhardy contestants might have made very good leads. But when Peter swaggered on the stage like a cowboy who'd been in the saddle for years, grinning as he sang the first lines of the opening song, it was obvious that here was the perfect Curley even if his own hair was rebelliously straight.

Suzy was willing to watch Melissa after half a dozen girls or so had tried for the part, but clapped her hand to her forehead as she remembered just in time that she had an appointment with the orthodontist, who had recently removed her braces. He never forgave anyone for being late but charged the fee whether the patient showed up or not. The rates for Suzy were reduced since her father was a dentist — a matter of professional courtesy — but even so her father vowed Suzy could have gone to college for what it had cost to have Dr. Robbins crochet wires around her teeth each week.

Suzy ran all the way to his office and barely got in under the wire (no pun intended).

"Mmm. You're going to be beautiful," Dr. Robbins said.

"When?" Suzy asked.

Dr. Robbins shrugged his shoulders. "Can't tell," he answered, unaware of the anxiety in her voice.

"You're changing, Suzanne Simmons, and I don't like it. I keep feeling that something is going on and you aren't telling us. And we don't see you anymore, not the way we used to, every day after school."

A mournful rainy Saturday. Patty, Mousie, and Suzy crouched before the enormous fireplace in the Morgan house. Patty was toasting marshmallows and placing them between slabs of chocolate and graham crackers, first offering one to Suzy and then to Mousie who stared at it and uttered the word "gross!" with such disgust that Patty sighed with discouragement.

For three afternoons now Suzy had slouched in the back of the auditorium, watching the tryouts and wishing she were one of them. She had seen the movie, *Oklahoma*, and loved it. As for the songs, she seemed to have always known them — "Oklahoma," "Oh, What a Beautiful Morning," "The Surrey with the Fringe on Top." At one time she would have been content to go to a performance, but now she would not rest until she was part of it. Why, even if she was the one who swept the stage after each performance after the audience went home, that would be almost enough. As it was, she feared she was left out, totally on the outside.

"I don't know what you're talking about," she answered Patty and Mousie. "I just don't understand what you mean by '*changing*.'"

"If there's something wrong, Suzy, maybe we can help. But you have to tell us about it," Patty said through a mouthful of cracker crumbs. Her blue eyes were wide with sympathy, the last thing Suzy wanted.

"There's nothing wrong, I tell you. Why should

I talk, talk, talk all the time?" Suzy shouted, standing up and pacing the long living room and ending her outburst with a crashing chord on the Morgans' grand piano. She was upset with herself for losing her temper, particularly when Patty was genuinely friendly and Mousie might have been too, yet she could not possibly tell them how she longed to be in *Oklahoma* and that she was hopelessly in love with Peter. Abashed, she sat on the cushion in front of the fire and picked up the marshmallow that had dropped out of her treat.

"I'm sorry," she said softly. She must remember that Patty too must suffer, or else she would not think of food so much and that Mousie must be unhappy too, or else she would not complain so much. She too was troubled and didn't know how to help them or herself.

For several minutes all three girls were quiet, watching the flames, and then Suzy, in a burst of genius, begged Mousie to read her latest murder mystery and so the three of them spent the rest of the afternoon swimming in a web of numerous, ingenious, and bloody murders.

Exactly one week after the tryouts began, all the parts were chosen and Suzy got up to leave the auditorium. There was no reason for her to feel disappointment, since she had not tried out for a part, yet she had half-suspected something unexpected and miraculous would happen. It didn't. Her posture was listless and her head hung down, so that she bumped into a tall red-headed girl who was pinning a notice to the bulletin board in the hall. Suzy begged her pardon, then lingered to read the notice.

HELP! HELP! (in urgent red brush strokes)
We need YOU to sew costumes for OKLA-
HOMA.
Yes, YOU and U and EWE
Come work with famed theater costumer, Ms.
Henry. Anyone who can sew anything at all is
welcome. Room 66 (Conference Room) after
school.

Make costumes! Suzy's eyes lit up. Of course,
that was something she could do.

Or could she? Memories of her sixth grade sewing teacher with a familiar refrain, "Rip it out,
Suzanne, and try it again." She recalled seams
bulging here and narrowing to nothing there, of
the right sleeve being placed in the left armhole and
vice versa so that she had the sensation of being in
a straitjacket when she wore that particular blouse,
and of a pocket sewed on perfectly but upside down.
If she had to prove her ability, she was lost. But
she had to be part of the costume crew. Perhaps
they would let her sew on buttons.

As she ran to Dr. Robbins, nearly late again, she
was thinking if she were making costumes, she would
get to see Peter at rehearsals. For that she would
learn to sew, no matter what it cost in mental or
physical anguish.

"And what are you grinning about today?" Dr.
Robbins asked. Suzy's smile widened, but she would
not tell.

Chapter 6

The following night after the first meeting of the Costume Crew, Suzy announced her news at the dinner table.

"You don't mean it! You're sewing, Suzy? Costumes that other people expect to wear?" Mrs. Simmons said.

"Great!" Suzy's father said, nodding his head and winking at her. Good Papa! "It's good to know how to sew. I had to learn sewing at dental school."

"Sewing up the inside of somebody's mouth. Ugh!" Cynthia made a face. That very thought made shivers go up and down Suzy's spine, but she said nothing since her father was proud of his stitching.

"It's nice to sew if you can't do anything else," Suzy's mother admitted, "but if it were me, I'd rather be on stage, dancing or singing or even being an extra. Sewing is so tiresome and besides nobody sews very much anymore."

"But they do, Mom. Some of those girls make

wonderful clothes for themselves. I wish I could sew like they do."

"You do? Remember that time you made a dress for Cynthia and she grew out of it before you finished it?"

"And there were all those dirty marks along the seams where you worked on it so much?" Cynthia added.

"But I was only in sixth grade then. I'm a different person now," Suzy insisted.

"Besides, if you work in the costume room," Suzy's mother went on, "you don't get credit for all the hard work you do. It's not fair, I know that, but you should know it too before you let yourself in for lots of hard, unrewarding work."

"That's not the point. It's not my ego that counts. It's being part of something bigger than you are, like in the Middle Ages when they built the big cathedrals. Hundreds of people worked on them, maybe thousands, but only one or two names were known. It's the work, it's the spirit that counts."

"H'm," Mrs. Simmons said. "Somebody must've given you a great pep talk."

"When I go to high school, I'm going to have the lead in every play," Cynthia announced, swooping up Marmaduke in her arms and walking away.

"Don't look so upset, Suzy. It's just that I hate to see you do all the work while everyone else gets the credit."

"Now, Evelyn!" said Dr. Simmons, while Suzy clapped her hands over her ears and went up to her bedroom.

After school that afternoon, Suzy had gone to Room 66, ordinarily a Conference Room, but now sporting a sloppy sign on the door, saying COS-TUME ROOM. Its chief virtue, as far as Suzy could see, was its location so close to the stage that it would be possible to hear what went on during the performance and with a little neck-straining watch it.

Eight girls beside herself showed up. Two of them, Jan and Lisa, thin, weedy girls who wore currently fashionable, full, gathered skirts remarkably well, had been the prize students in the sixth grade sewing class in which Suzy was clearly the class dunce. At that time they were working with Vogue Designer patterns while Suzy was still struggling with Project One, a pot holder.

"I remember you from sixth grade," Lisa said. "In fact, I'll never forget you."

"Are you really here to SEW?" Jan asked.

Suzy lifted her head and turned the other way, obviously insulted. A bad beginning.

Of the other girls in the room, two were seniors who had tried out for OKLAHOMA and hadn't made it; three were innocent gum-chewers and chatterers; and the last was a quiet wraith of a girl who sat with averted eyes and said nothing. None of them paid attention to Suzy, who moved to a seat in the far corner of the room.

The next bit of discouraging news was that Miss Pritchett, the sewing teacher, promised to oversee the Costume Crew part of the time, for Suzy saw in the tight, pinched mouth, the thin, turned-up nose, the neat, graying coiffure from which a hair would not dare to stray, one of that small tidy breed of teacher who would not be able to stand Suzy. She could already hear the high nasal voice sighing, "No, Suzanne, that seam is simply not straight. If you will rip it from here to there and begin again . . . no wait, you'd better rip that seam too and do the sleeve over again."

"I might as well get up and leave now," Suzy was thinking.

And then Ms. Henry, mother of Veronica, who was taking the part of Ado Annie, breezed into the room and beamed at everyone.

"So this is our crew! Isn't that wonderful! You are all wonderful to come. We are going to have a great experience together!"

How inspiring she was, Suzy thought, the most self-confident woman she had ever seen. It was clear that she was connected to the 'the-a-tuh' — actually The Elmwood Heights Little Theater — as she perched on the edge of the oak table and chatted with the Costume Crew. Longish hair tucked under an apricot-colored silk scarf, dangling gold earrings, eight gold chains and African beads dangling around a low cut silk shirt, and pants tucked into high, tan boots. Suzy was wishing her mother would dress like that just once, but doubted that she would. However, Suzy decided, that is more or less how she would like to dress. She would also like to have the low, husky voice that Ms. Henry used so well.

"Some people think that making costumes is only sewing, but they are wrong. Believe me, they don't know. Costumes are *creations*. Where would an actor be without a costume? Imagine *Oklahoma* without costumes. . . it simply would not be the same. The one who makes the costume creates the play. Never forget that."

Suzy was sitting straighter now, even leaning forward a little.

"You all know the *ambiance* of the musical. The atmosphere should be fresh, countrylike, sprightly, pure as sweet butter and buttercups. . . ."

She could have gone on in this vein for several pages, but the sound of sawing, which rather made Suzy's teeth ache, interrupted her. Suzy looked out of the window and saw that Daniel Bright, along with two girls and a boy, was sawing large pieces of plywood in two.

"There, they are already beginning on the scenery. Isn't that wonderful?" Ms. Henry went on. "We'll be working too, very soon now. Let me show you the sketches. Remember, the play takes place right after the turn of the century and we'll want the right things: checkered shirts, jeans, and chaps for the cowboys, and of course, straw hats. As for the girls, flouncy dresses in muslins, calico, percale, and broadcloth, with all kinds of trimmings. And of course, petticoats."

Immediately Jan, Lisa, and the others, even the very quiet girl, began to discuss materials, ruffles, jabots, gores. . .all of this practically a foreign language to Suzy who wore pants, tee shirts, and occasionally her beloved, ragged, and somewhat outgrown jean skirt. Ms. Henry passed the sketches she had drawn for the costumes and while everyone swooned over them, Suzy gulped. They were beautiful, but to think of sewing anything so complex left her with her mouth open in astonishment. How would one begin? Possibly she should have slipped out then. But Ms. Henry was talking.

". . .and Curley, that is Peter, will be in blues most of the time, but girls, wait until you see his wedding shirt! I haven't quite finished drawing it yet. And here's Melissa's. . .I mean Laurie's. . .wedding dress. Isn't that a beauty? And don't forget, we have to sew the clothes in the peddler's pack, the red flannel drawers, and other goodies. We're going to have fun here, I tell you. Any questions?"

Miss Pritchett was beginning to spoil the fun. "How many costumes in all do we make?" she asked.

"Well, I haven't finished counting them all, because we'll need petticoats and unless the boys come up with their own shirts. . .possibly ninety-two anyway, and more. I'm afraid there'll be more. There always is."

Immediately Suzy divided nine into ninety-two. Would she be responsible then for a little over ten costumes before March 20th? But how could she possibly do that when it had taken her three months to make a pot holder when she was in the sixth grade?

There, she was biting her thumb, a dreadful habit which was probably responsible for her having had to go through orthodontistry and wear those ugly braces, but when she became nervous, it was somehow comforting to bite her thumb. Possibly she should give up now before she began.

And then a ripple of notes came from the slightly out-of-tune piano on the stage and immediately following that the sound of Peter's voice, high and clear. It was heaven to hear it. Suzy was loving the play, loving the sound of live music, the vitality of Peter's voice. She could not quit now.

"Will somebody please shut that door so we can hear ourselves think?" Miss Pritchett whined. Lisa rolled her eyes and closed the door. Then Miss Pritchett held up a board on which were pinned examples of seams, bastings, rufflings, hemming, and such, almost all of them more complex than Suzy remembered. "Remember girls," Miss Pritchett was saying as she finished her introductory lecture, "I can't be with you every day. Only once in a while."

Suzy tried not to smile too broadly or cheer out loud. Her head was full of Peter singing OOOOOOOklahoma, and all the way home she hummed it. Mr. Rodgers and Mr. Hammerstein probably never imagined, when they wrote it, that that song, sung by Peter, would one day turn Suzy into a seamstress.

Chapter 7

Suzy found backstage life exhilarating. Within days she became entirely immersed in the play and lived in an *Oklahoma* world. Like the others in the costume room who repeated the lines spoken on stage, Suzy sometimes caught herself talking with a western twang, saying "pertaters and termaters," "Yeow!" and "Paw and Maw" which did not ring kindly on the ears of Dr. and Mrs. Simmons.

"Ah jist cain't he'p it," she said.

At breakfast once, her father had the misfortune to say, "It's a nice day!" Immediately Suzy picked up the cue and sang "Oh, what a beautiful mornin'! Oh, what a beautiful day!"

Cynthia stuck her fingers in her ears and closed her eyes tight while Mrs. Simmons frowned.

When corn was served at dinner, Suzy saw it not as boiled nuggets that had until five minutes ago been frozen, but fields of corn "high as an elephant's eye!"

"Suzy, will you have more stew?" her mother asked. An irresistible cue.

Softly, Suzy answered in Ado Annie's song. "I'm jist a girl who cain't say no!"

Sighs of exasperation around the table, yet Dr. Simmons grinned. Was it possible his daughter was changing? She seemed so much lighter these days.

"How long does this play go on?" Mrs. Simmons asked.

"Forever, I hope," Suzy answered.

It would be difficult to assess how many people were responsible for making the costumes. Some of the crew stayed away for as long as a week and then showed. Occasionally a member of the cast strolled in and offered to sew on buttons or help in any other way. Jan and Lisa took on the most responsibility for the costumes, although they took alternating afternoons off. Only one person showed up every day for two or three hours. Suzy. "Wouldn't you know *she'd* be the one?" Miss Pritchett whispered to Jan.

Suzy was allowed to do all the basting, since it was thought she would do least harm that way. When she concentrated on it, she basted very well, but if she began to dream of Peter, which happened frequently, then the thread mysteriously tied itself into knots, or she tended to baste her own skirt in with the material.

One day when there was more need for hemming than basting, she was taught to hem and amazed herself as well as the others by hemming properly with delicate, even stitches. Thereafter the hemming was saved for her. Suzy was delighted, for she did not feel constrained to sit in the Costume Room but could wander to the wings and watch the rehearsals while she hemmed.

And so she found out how the play was slowly put together and more importantly how Peter worked. For all the apparent ease of his manner, he worked more doggedly than anyone, for he was a perfectionist, even more so than Mr. Rossetti. One day when Peter tried a new bit of stage business, entering by jumping over a rail fence, he insisted on doing it over and over until he accomplished exactly the easy grace he wanted. Everyone else waited, some of the chorus sighing and saying, "There he is, at it again. We'll be here forever."

But Suzy's eyes were bright, for she thought it a remarkable trait, the sign of a genuine artist.

One afternoon as she stood in the wings, hemming a petticoat, she found a new fantasy as Peter and Melissa sang "People Will Say We're in Love." Melissa suffered a terrible pain and was rushed off to the hospital for an immediate operation, nothing tragic but serious enough to keep her from being in the play. Where would they find another Laurie? Mr. Rossetti, Peter, everyone would look around, and suddenly Peter would blink his eyes. "Here, I think this could work. . ." He would drag Suzy on the stage, the piano would play softly, and she would find herself singing the duet with Peter, "People will say we're in love!" Of course she could act; of course she could dance and sing; all it would take was someone who believed in her. She would be transformed; she would even become a kind of legend, a Cinderella.

It was during one of these daydreaming sessions that she experienced a mean little pinch on her arm. Miss Pritchett.

"I didn't mean to hurt you, Suzy, but I've been talking to you for the last five minutes and you didn't seem to hear. We need that petticoat you're hemming now. Kathie's here to try it on. Is it finished? Let's see what you've done. Five inches in half an hour? Is that all?"

Shamefaced Suzy followed Miss Pritchett back to the Costume Room and heard a lecture about the advisability of working there and not backstage. Lisa had piled nine costumes that had to be ripped and resewn for one reason or another (Suzy's efforts being the most obvious reason) and so Suzy sat in the corner by the window and ripped. Outside the scene crew was assembling what would be the porch of a ranch house. Daniel Bright was measuring a door frame, felt someone looking at him, and turning around grinned up at Suzy, reddened, then returned to his hammer and nails.

"Don't worry about hurrying," Miss Pritchett said sarcastically. "We only have eighty costumes left to do."

In a whisper that Suzy could not help overhearing, Miss Pritchett urged Lisa and Jan to pin parts together very carefully so that Suzy could not possibly again make the mistake of sewing the front of a calico skirt to the back of a striped skirt, an event from which Miss Pritchett had not yet recovered. Suzy, cheeks burning, worked steadily, vowing that one day she would make Miss Pritchett eat her words. She would make the most beautiful dress with all the ruffles and flounces Lisa and Jan produced so easily.

Work had not yet begun on the finest dress of all, Laurie's wedding dress, but it was Peter's wedding shirt that excited Suzy. As soon as Miss Pritchett left, Suzy spoke to Lisa who had begun to put the parts of Peter's shirt together.

"Is that the wedding shirt that Curley wears? Lisa, would you let me sew on it, please? Anything at all. I'll be careful."

Bobbie, one of the senior girls, snickered. "There's another one falling for the great hero."

"That's not it, really," Suzy said. "He's a good actor. He's never been better."

"When did you ever see him before?" Jan asked.

Suzy faltered. Peter had appeared in her dreams for so long, it seemed as though she had always known him.

"Don't feel bad," Nan, the other senior, said. "Everyone falls madly in love with Peter. It's the thing to do. You'll get over it."

"Who's *in love*? Not me," Suzy said loudly, bending over the skirt she was basting for the third time.

"Don't be embarrassed," Nan continued. "It's like a childhood disease, falling for Peter. Lisa will let you sew on the buttons, won't you, Lis?"

Suzy bent over her work in silence, working the needle in and out furiously. For a moment, while the girls chattered, she glanced out of the window. Three girls were painting a large backdrop and Daniel seemed to be directing a new construction, referring to blueprints in his hand and measuring planks. Apparently he had delegated the finishing of the porch to a girl in overalls.

"Now there has to be the most serious dude in the school," Nan said.

"And the shyest," Lisa said. "Even if you look vaguely in his direction, he gets flustered."

"He blushes but he doesn't get flustered," Suzy said, wondering why she should defend him so forcefully. The other girls giggled, either because something about Daniel struck them as being funny, or they had been locked up in the Costume Room too long.

Not three minutes later, Daniel came in, a paint chip in his hand.

"Yes, can we help you?" Lisa asked, her face red with suppressed laughter.

"We're painting the backdrop for the first act and we've got to get the right shade so that the backdrop won't clash with the costumes. Could you show me some of the costumes?"

"Maybe Suzy would like to let you see them," Nan said, winking at Lisa.

Without a word, Suzy went to the rack where the costumes hung and Daniel followed. In a voice so low it was nearly inaudible, she pointed out Laurie's dress, a cornflower blue, and the dresses the dancers would wear.

"Terrific! Would you have a scrap of leftover material I could have? I think the paint will have to be somewhat deepened."

"Sure," Lisa said, finding a few strips of leftover material. "Are you a little sentimental about Laurie's dress?"

"Sentimental?" Daniel asked, puzzled. "Why would I be sentimental? The backdrop has to be exactly done or it won't work. The colors have to vibrate."

Jan, Lisa, and Nan burst into uncontrollable giggles and Suzy, embarrassed for them, covered the situation by reaching for even more scraps of dresses that appeared in the first act.

"Don't mind them," she whispered. "They are having fits, that's all. Stir crazy."

He winked at her quickly, then turned to the others. "Thanks," he said. Then, betrayed by a sudden reddening of his face, he left.

"You hurt his feelings," Suzy said. "He thought you were laughing at him."

"But we were, and then we weren't, not really. There's something funny about him."

"Well, I don't see it that way at all. Even so, you hurt his feelings. Don't you care?"

Everything was going wrong. She picked up her sewing and left, going into the wings.

This time since the scene rehearsed did not require Peter, he sat in the first row of the auditorium, watching the play, his blue eyes serious and intent on the other actors. He relaxed, like an animal at rest, his long legs stretched out in front of him. Again, as if it occurred to her for the first time, she murmured, "He's beautiful, beautiful."

When she was finished, she decided that this was the time to satisfy her curiosity about where Peter lived. Since there was only one Gilbert in the telephone book, she thought that the address given there, 47 Cassidy Lane, must be the place, on the opposite side of town from where she lived. She decided to go then, knowing that the long rehearsal meant he would probably not be there and so wouldn't discover her riding around streets where she didn't belong.

Forty-seven Cassidy Lane, in the "old" part of town where the streets curved and sometimes disappeared altogether, turned out to be a small, cramped house, painted an indifferent yellow and trimmed with a particularly cheap imitation brick. A modest, ordinary house in need of fresh paint. The yard boasted three stunted evergreens, one of which appeared to be dying. Volunteer grass grew in patches and a low fence was broken in one place and never repaired.

"So that's it!" she said.

She pedaled home slowly. Wasn't it amazing, she asked herself, that a "white knight," a person as elegant and gifted as Peter, should come from such a dreary home, whereas she, Suzy, as plain and talentless as a girl could be, should now be riding to that new pretentious home in what her mother called "the right side of Elmwood Heights" with its garden and terrace and the doorbell that rang "Tea for Two."

Chapter 8

Then something strange began to happen. It
came about so gradually that long before the evidence showed, there was a disquieting feeling that
something was not quite right. But what?

At first, when rehearsals began, the pace was
leisurely, as if there were all the time in the world.
The orchestra practiced alone in the music room;
the dancers worked out routines in the gym; and
the actors gradually worked out entrances, exits,
and the more subtle demands of timing and action.
As the time for performance grew near and the
orchestra, chorus, dancers, and actors rehearsed
together, blending their parts, excitement mounted,
even among those in the Costume Room.

"I have never seen a better production," Nan
said. "Everything is going GREAT! Everyone
working together."

Suzy wanted to keep her from going on. Such
words were bad luck, bound to tempt the fates. She
herself believed it was so, but, of course, she could
not compare this with any other production, never

having been involved with another play. And yet she sensed an undercurrent of something disagreeable, something she could not understand.

It wasn't the Costume Room that was in trouble, nor was she. In fact, as the pressure to finish the costumes mounted, she graduated from basting and hemming to more intricate jobs. To her amazement either the necessity of finishing ninety costumes (and more!) or a decision to show Miss Pritchett that she could sew, brought about an improvement in her skills that amazed her. Why, she could cut out shirts, put in zippers without breaking the machine needle, gather ruffles evenly, and accomplish other miracles. She had sewed the buttons on Curley's wedding shirt and when the time came, she would sew the hem and place the ribbons on the most important costume of all, Laurie's wedding dress.

That mysterious trouble, whatever it was, did not lie in the Costume Room. Ms. Henry came in almost every day now to praise everyone and encourage them. On one occasion she even hugged Suzy for doing so well.

Nor did the difficulty lie with the Stage Crew. Although the director had said it was too difficult to construct a surrey with a fringe on top, Daniel refused to accept defeat and accomplished it. He had found wheels in an old barn somewhere off in Sonoma County, and had insisted on going ahead with it. Every day Suzy watched its progress. If only she could do something with wood, why. . .she could remake her whole bedroom. Maybe someday. After all, if she could put in a zipper, there was no telling how far she might go.

The orchestra, the chorus, and the dancers improved each day. What then was that underlying sensation that something was wrong? At first it was undefinable, a stirring, a faint sense of something not quite right. Even Mr. Rossetti was concerned, frowning, and running his fingers through what would have been his hair if it had not disappeared long ago.

"Let's do that scene again. It doesn't quite come across!" he said to Peter and Melissa.

Since Miss Pritchett had not come that day, Suzy stood in the wings and tacked ricrac on Aunt Eller's apron, and so witnessed what happened.

Peter and Melissa were singing a duet, "People Will Say We're in Love," and Suzy was humming along with them, when suddenly Melissa stopped singing and stamped her foot so loud that Suzy jumped.

"You're upstaging me, Peter Gilbert. Mr. Rossetti," she appealed to the director, "he moves back all the time so that I have to keep my back toward the audience. Otherwise it looks stupid."

"Why, Mr. Rossetti, I wouldn't dream of upstaging Melissa. I need room to breathe when I sing. I need space. But upstage Melissa? Never," Peter said with an air of convincing innocence.

"Come now. At this stage of the game do I have to chalk out the places where you're supposed to stand? You know better, but I'll do it anyway." He jumped on the stage and clearly marked the floor with chalk. "Peter, you stand here. Melissa, there. Now, once more!"

"There they go again, another fight," Nan said. She too had seen the fracas.

"You mean that Melissa and Peter have fought before in other plays? But they're both so good," Suzy said.

"That's exactly the trouble," Nan said. "Green eyes. Jealousy. You get it?"

The rehearsal continued. The tiff, for that's all it seemed, had not lasted long and everyone enjoyed it. Still Suzy thought she detected a certain iciness in Melissa's voice and Peter overacted, singing too loudly. Suzy convinced herself it was simply a minor incident. Jealousy was such a mean characteristic, she could not believe Peter so petty as to be guilty of it.

The next day it happened again. Melissa stopped in the middle of another duet. "Mr. Rossetti, I'm standing where the chalk marks are and that baboon is standing two feet in back of his line."

"Mr. Rossetti, I swear. . ." Peter protested.

"Cut it, both of you! No more of this nonsense. It's equal billing here. Time you thought about the play. Peter, watch it. Melissa, don't be so sensitive. Okay. Once more."

This time the tenseness was unmistakable as they practically hissed the song. Suzy actually saw Peter making a face at Melissa and Melissa flounced around the stage with a haughtiness that could not be anything but insulting.

Maybe he doesn't like her after all, Suzy thought.

The flare-ups continued, and now the girls from the Costume Room gathered to see what would happen next, and the Production Crew hung around to watch. Suzy was hardly proud of herself for enjoying the spectacle, yet like everyone else, she wondered what they would do next.

But why had it happened? Suzy figured it out. They were too much alike and so they were not right for each other, not in the least. It was opposites that attracted, not equals. Well then, if anyone was completely different from Melissa, it was Suzy. And so. . .

Suzy's dream was not noble but she was discovering a possibility. It was the male bird that developed the bright flashy plumage, while the female remained modest, brown, and quiet. Since it was a matter of nature, then the same theory might hold for human beings too. And so if a girl wanted Peter to like her, then it would be foolish to try to compete with Melissa, imitating her clothes or the way she walked, swaying her hips and shoulders so that the eyes of every boy followed her every movement. No, it would be wiser to be gentle and modest. If only Peter noticed her, then he would know that Suzy would always admire him, would never upstage him, or flounce about in a fit of temper. A Suzy could not act on the stage with him, but she could be waiting for him in the wings. After the play, it would be her applause he would want. Melissa, showy as she was, would be looking out for herself.

A new fantasy grew. Peter noticed her, suddenly understood her, realized how fine she was, and gave up Melissa forever. He would even ask her to the Spring Dance which was one of the big senior dances, second only to the prom. What a coup it would be, Suzy dancing in Peter's arms!

Miss Pritchett had come into the Costume Room, but Suzy had not noticed. Now she shrieked. "Good heavens, look what you've done!"

Suzy had been hemming the extravagant ruffle on the bottom of Laurie's wedding dress and had not even noticed that she had pricked her finger with the needle, staining the bottom of the dress with blood, a handsome red hue. How symbolic, Suzy thought.

"Quick, bring some cold water!" Miss Pritchett cried.

Suzy picked up a discarded Coke container, rushed to the drinking fountain and returned with the water. Miss Pritchett plunged the stained ruffle into the water and immediately the blood dissolved, leaving only a faint yellowish ring. Suzy almost fainted with relief that the dress would be all right, when Miss Pritchett remembered something else.

"Anyone have a Band-Aid? We'll have to do something about that finger. First thing you know, you'll get an infection and maybe they'll have to saw off the finger, or even the hand or the arm if it gets gangrene. It can start just from something simple like this. And then the school gets sued. There's no end of trouble. . ."

At the thought of losing a finger or an arm, Suzy truly did feel faint and had to sit down. Lisa managed to find some Band-Aids in a first-aid box in the gym, and Miss Pritchett muttered as she put it on.

"Maybe you've done enough for today, Suzy. Want to go home?"

If she finished the sentence, she would have added "go home and don't come back again." Suzy would have left, but Peter was scheduled to come in and try on his shirt. "Please, it's only a needle prick and it's not as if I go around bleeding all the time."

"Well," Miss Pritchett gave in. "Better work on these red flannel drawers then and let someone else do the wedding dress."

Nervous with excitement because Peter would

soon show up in the Costume Room, Suzy combed her hair, applied a touch of blusher to her cheeks, and picked up the red flannel drawers with some distaste. It was hardly what she would have chosen to work on when Peter made his entrance.

At last he came. From the stool in the corner where she sat, Suzy watched Peter take off the white gauzy shirt he liked to wear and put on the wedding shirt while Lisa and Jan fussed about, pinning and tucking, and making sure that the fit was perfect. Peter smiled pleasantly, but it was clear his mind was somewhere else. At one unexpected moment, he grinned at Suzy, at which she became almost as red as the flannel drawers she was basting. But then he had grinned at everyone, even Miss Pritchett.

"We're finished," Jan said, and Lisa helped Peter take off the shirt. Suzy noticed how honey brown and warm his skin was, how slender and yet strong was his chest. He put on his gauze shirt, buttoned the cuffs but let the top remain open. He was perfect, perfect. She thought the young Greek gods must have looked like this.

"Thanks," Peter said casually and went back to the stage. Suzy sat open-mouthed and for five minutes or more forgot she was supposed to be sewing.

Chapter 9

At dinner that evening Dr. and Mrs. Simmons were discussing guests they planned to invite to a party later that month. "What about Bob Blanc?" Dr. Simmons asked. "Haven't seen him for ages."

"Great," Mrs. Simmons said, "I want to see his new wife. Irene, is it? I've got to see who's followed Gloria's act."

"Very different," Dr. Simmons said. "A little wren, quiet, small, brownish. Nothing like Gloria. And she thinks that Bob is the most wonderful man in the world. What a change!"

Suzy, who had been dawdling over a tuna casserole, sat up with sudden interest. Was this another proof of her theory of opposites? Bob, one of her father's friends, a brilliant, attractive man had been married to Gloria, a brilliant, attractive woman who ran an art gallery and gift shop. Suzy had agreed with her mother that Gloria was too extravagant and showy for Elmwood Heights and sure enough, like a rare orchid that must exist in the right environment, Gloria flew off to Los Angeles and divorced a broken-hearted Robert who remarried within three months.

"And he's happy with his new wife?" Mrs. Simmons asked.

"Divinely. He's a changed and changing man. You'll see," Dr. Simmons said.

The formula worked, Suzy was thinking. Of course it was not marriage that would concern her for years and years, but simply the way people worked out. Important, handsome men needed quiet, large-eyed, adoring girls. Of course, she would be much better for Peter than Melissa. If only Peter knew...

Unexpectedly the rehearsals for *Oklahoma*, which had been going so well, began to falter. Nearly half the dancers came down with flu, much of it being the "ski-flu" variety, since this was the last chance to go skiing that season. Other members of the cast had jobs they had to go to, and so missed half of each rehearsal. As for the costumes, someone had miscounted and twenty more had still to be made.

As if that weren't enough, the feud between Peter and Melissa was escalating, mounting in intensity from day to day. Unfortunately the in-fighting became fully as interesting as the play itself, and everyone who could waited in the wings to see what would happen next.

One day Peter jumped up with a cry of pain. "I'm sorry, Mr. Rossetti, but she came down on my foot with those heels of hers."

"Who, me?" Melissa asked with a wide, green-eyed innocence, so exaggerated that they practically boasted of her guilt as she then gazed down fondly at the spikey heels of her boots.

"Let's try it again, and, Joe, get me an Alka-Seltzer," Mr. Rossetti asked of his assistant stage manager.

The next day Suzy saw three of the cowboys in the cast giggling and crowding around Peter who was eating half a sandwich. She was able to conclude that the filling was pure onion. During the duets, he held Melissa close to him and sang in her face, so that she had to blow away the fumes.

She retaliated the next day by slicing three cloves of garlic into the hot dog she had for lunch.

Not to be outdone, Peter resorted to putting tabasco sauce on his lips. It did not bother him, but he knew that Melissa's lips were sensitive, and so they burned throughout the rehearsal, although she refused to give him the satisfaction of crying out with discomfort.

More tricks? The next time Peter took off his Western straw hat with a flourish, gracefully covering Melissa's face at a time when they would be expecting applause.

Then she upstaged him, taking him by surprise.

The next trick backfired. As Peter danced with Melissa, he twirled her around with such force that she fell and got up rubbing her posterior.

"Perfect, perfect!" Mr. Rossetti called out. "A great piece of stage business. Keep it in. Peter, don't hurt the girl, just pretend to be so carried away you become unintentionally rough. Melissa, you were terrific!"

"Mr. Rossetti, that *hurts*!" she complained, rubbing the sore part.

"Art doesn't come cheap," Mr. Rossetti consoled her.

"Do you think they're really sore with each other, I mean Peter and Melissa, or do you think they're just playing games, faking it?" Suzy asked Nan when they returned to the Costume Room from the wings.

"I don't know," she said, "but I think that what they're doing is more fun than the whole blinking play."

"It's like a play within a play," another girl said.

Suzy didn't know what to say. She had to admit it was exciting. Half the girls in the Costume Room were on Peter's side and half on Melissa's. Suzy was beginning to worry about *Oklahoma*, which was clearly suffering from the feud, yet she had to admit, it *was* fascinating.

She decided the feud must be genuine. Peter never appeared with Melissa as he walked through the corridors, but either strode by himself or walked with his old buddies. Suzy, passing them, heard snatches of conversation about sports or about who was taking who to the Spring Dance. Twice Peter saw Suzy and smiled, said "Hi" and walked right on.

Melissa had never acknowledged Suzy's existence by as much as a nod. Now she ambled down the hall with two or three friends or the football captain, Al Sakovich, with whom she smiled toothily and laughed loudly and frequently.

It was small of Suzy and not at all in keeping with her character to find hope in this. She wished no harm to Melissa, but the feud did seem to remove an enormous obstacle from her path, whatever that was!

Of course it didn't help to walk to school with Patty and Mousie.

"I think that Melissa Schmerz is just wonderful, don't you, Suzy? I can't wait to see her in *Oklahoma*. I hear she's in love with Peter and he's in love with her. Don't you think that's romantic?"

"No," Suzy said. "Not in the least."

"BUT," Mousie said, ready to argue. Whenever she began a sentence with a big BUT, Suzy was ready to shake her. "Schmerz is talented. She's going to be a star someday."

"What about Peter?" Suzy asked. "Have you ever seen him or heard him sing?"

"He's okay," Mousie admitted, "BUT, Schmerz has the talent."

So, Suzy thought, they worshipped Melissa. Traitors, both of them!

Now that Melissa had become more Peter's enemy than his friend, new daydreams and fantasies created themselves in Suzy's head. But unlike the other dreams which inevitably took place in Paris or Hollywood or San Francisco, these were closer to Elmwood Heights. She saw Peter approaching her in the wings and talking with her; she saw him coming to the Costume Room on the pretext of seeing her, asking her if she would sew on a button that was in danger of coming loose; she saw herself in a long dress, dancing with him at the Spring Dance!

* * *

"Suzanne Simmons, from now on I want to see you in the Costume Room. You spend entirely too much time out there in the wings and we have too much to do," Miss Pritchett said. "We have costume fittings all week now."

That was the exciting part, as the dancers and the girls in the chorus came in to be dressed and fitted. Melissa squealed with delight over the costumes that had been made for her and hugged both Jan and Lisa enthusiastically. How phony she is, Suzy thought, and yet it couldn't be denied that she bubbled with vitality. She was Someone, a full ten on Suzy's scale. Suzy's spirits, which went up and down like a yo-yo, now dropped considerably and refused to rise. She was hopeless, hopeless. Her rating of herself dropped to one, the lowest yet.

In fact she became so depressed that she almost missed being aware that someone was tapping her shoulder. She turned to see Daniel Bright.

"I was wondering, would you like to see the sets? They're all backstage now, and we need an opinion from someone who hasn't been working on them," he said.

"I see," she said. "Sure, I'd love to see them."

Poor Daniel, she thought. He had to make the invitation businesslike although what he was really saying was, come and see the wonderful things we've made.

"Terrific! Wonderful!" she said, sincerely enough, since she had not imagined the sets could be so convincing. The rail fence, the porch, the grove, the ranch, and most of all the surrey were perfectly designed and made.

"It's all so professional," she said, "and the backdrop, that wide blue sky, is gorgeous, with that one little cloud."

"Come and look at it closely," he said leading her to the cloud. Only when she was very close to it, could she see that a tiny flying saucer had been painted in it. She laughed.

"I love it. It's delightful."

"Now we should see the set from the back of the auditorium," he said. "Would you mind? In case something is wrong, we still have time to fix it."

They walked up the aisle to the back. "It's even better from here," Suzy said. "It's a perfect June sky. It looks as if it would go on forever and ever."

Suddenly she wished she were in Oklahoma, not the production, but Oklahoma as it was at the turn of the century, when everything seemed so much simpler. But here she was in Elmwood Heights High and it was time to get back to the Costume Room.

"Daniel, I don't think it can be improved. Really. It's perfect."

He frowned. He blushed. He coughed a little. But she knew he was pleased.

"Miss Pritchett will kill me," she explained.

"Then let's go back," he said, and silently they walked down the aisle.

Miss Pritchett was indeed furious. "Where've you been? Suzy, we need you. Can you come back tonight after dinner? Can you work Saturday?"

Suzy had promised to coach Kate Osborne for a math test, but Kate would have to wait.

"Do you really need me?" Suzy asked, her eyes gleaming.

"We most certainly do," Miss Pritchett snapped.

Suzy could have hugged her. That was proof then that she was wanted. Her rating shot up to four. Or four and a half.

Mrs. Simmons pretended to be annoyed when Suzy came home late for dinner and announced she would be sewing all weekend.

"I can't believe it. Suzy sewing. I can't imagine you sewing so much," Mrs. Simmons said.

"Or at all," Cynthia added.

"That's how it is. I can do practically everything now. And they need me, they really do. Even Miss Prissy Pritchett said so."

"Bravo!" Dr. Simmons said. "If everyone had spirit like Suzy, this country would be out of trouble in a hurry."

"I was hoping we could all go to the city on Saturday," Suzy's mother said regretfully. "Can't you come? We'll be going out for dinner."

"Oooo, I'd love it," Suzy cried, and then shook her head, "but some other time. All right?"

Chapter 10

"And now dress rehearsal's clutching at our throats!" Ms. Henry announced.

"It's so sudden," Suzy said and everyone agreed, even though they had known since early January that eventually it would come. Rehearsals of the last week had taken a downward turn and there was talk of *Oklahoma* being jinxed. One dancer broke her toe and at the last minute a less than promising substitute had to be used. Part of the scenery, some trees in the grove scene, kept falling over and Daniel was at his wit's end, trying to get them to stand up.

"Everything's against us!" someone cried out loud. Even the weather threatened unexpected and heavy rains as storm clouds glowered over Elmwood Heights.

However, it was the feud between Peter and Melissa that was undermining the spirit of the play. On the surface, their roles were satisfactory but less sparkling than before. The tricks went on almost as if Peter and Melissa could no longer help themselves and the worst part was that they were so fascinating that now everyone, even Miss Pritchett, stood in the wings to see what new piece of nastiness they could make up. A play within a play.

"So this is what dress rehearsal is like. Wow!" Suzy thought, breaking off a piece of thread with her teeth. Now came the last minute costumer's work as she resewed a seam that had split in the last rehearsal. Dancers ran back and forth backstage, stretching and warming up. Members of the chorus walked through the auditorium and backstage, practicing scales and arpeggios. The orchestra seemed to consist of thirty musicians, each playing a private solo regardless of what anyone else was doing. Backstage the cowboys couldn't resist swinging their lariats as they tried to lasso the girls in the chorus.

The Costume Room was in a dither. Someone had stolen the red flannel drawers that had to appear in the peddler's pack, and a new pair had to be stitched up at the last minute. Buttons that had popped off had to be resewn and people kept coming in with minor complaints. . .a ribbon had fallen off, a hem had become undone, one of the cowboy's pants had split and needed first aid.

A big crowd hung around the Makeup Room, formerly a classroom, where one of the girls was curling Peter's straight hair with an electric curling iron. There was no end of joking. For all that had to be done in the Costume Room, still Suzy escaped and stood on tiptoe at the back of the crowd, to catch a glimpse of Peter with curls.

"Well, it's supposed to be confusing and exciting," Ms. Henry said about the dress rehearsal, "but I tell you, those two leads can spoil the whole thing. They're supposed to be in love and they sing to each other like two cats getting their back up and spatting. A bad business."

"Maybe it will be all right," Suzy said in a soft, hopeful voice. She could not bear to think of the play being spoiled. Even if it meant that Peter and Melissa would have to make up and end her fantasies, she would still prefer the play to go well. After all, where did fantasies and daydreams lead? Only to more of the same.

The rehearsal started late and badly, with one mishap after another. The curtain refused to part and the orchestra had to play the same phrase over and over eight times until the ropes were adjusted.

Then one of the dancer's skirts fell off. Suzy clapped her hands over her mouth. Had she not put the fasteners on right or had the dancer not used them correctly?

One of the cowboys jumped over the rail fence but missed it, sending it clattering down to the floor.

Finally the first violinist in the orchestra, playing an especially touching solo, cried out an explosive and unmistakable DAMN! when his E string broke.

"What else can possibly happen now?" Mr. Rossetti cried, half collapsing in his seat halfway back in the auditorium.

"Typical, typical!" Ms. Henry said under her

breath as she stood in the wings with the rest of the costume crew. Now two dancers entered from the right side of the stage instead of the left, confusing the girls who were already performing so that half the dancers collided with one another. Ms. Henry covered her eyes and shook her head at the disaster.

But it was the duet between Curley and Laurie that everyone awaited. Oddly enough it seemed to be going beautifully. They sang well, they even appeared to be quite in love.

"But somep'n's gonna happen," one of the cowboys in the wings said.

"Cain't keep it back," another said.

"An' it's gonna be a beaut!" a third one chimed in.

Yet nothing happened where they were concerned until near the very end when everyone was ready to heave a sigh of relief that at least nothing seemed to be going wrong for them. Peter put his arm around Melissa as they sang, and never had they sung more beautifully, when suddenly Melissa doubled up with a hysterical laugh which she could not stop. Then, laughing no more, she stood up, face red with fury, and slapped Peter first on one cheek and then the other, hard brutal slaps which could be heard in the farthest corners of the auditorium.

"You creep!" she yelled. "You dirty double-crossing creep."

Peter stood back speechless, arms folded, his face a mask.

"What's going on *now*, for heaven's sake?" Mr. Rossetti shrieked.

"He tickled me, Mr. Rossetti. He knows I'm fatally ticklish and he did it on purpose."

"Mr. Rossetti, that's a total lie. If I touched her in a sensitive place, it was accidental," Peter said, practically crossing his heart to protest his innocence. A ho-ho-ho from the wings brought a weak chorus of snickers. "I won't take being assaulted like that."

"Look," Mr. Rossetti said, his voice dangerously low and calm. "You both make me sick. You think you're stars, the only ones in this play, but there are more than a hundred people who have been working as hard as you and you're about to spoil all their work. Do you realize that?"

Melissa stood still, eyes lowered, as if penitent.

"I'm sorry," Peter said. "I apologize for anything I did that could have spoiled the play. I'll settle my private score with Melissa outside, I mean it. But while I'm on stage, I'll do everything I can to make *Oklahoma* work."

"I'm sorry too," Melissa said. "If he behaves, we won't have any trouble at all."

They sang the last duet once more, this time without trickery, but it was clear that Peter, cheeks flaming, was still furious with Melissa.

"He really is going to get even with her," Jan said. "Just look at him."

"I'll say," said one of the boys on the lighting crew. "I've seen that cat lose his temper, but never like this."

As the final curtain came down, Peter, whose arms had been around Melissa, jumped back from her as if she were a snake.

"You can just forget about me taking you to

the Spring Dance. I wouldn't take you to a cat-fight. I'd ask anyone in this school, rather than take you."

Melissa shrugged her shoulders as if she didn't care, jumped down from the surrey and tapped her foot impatiently as she waited for Mr. Rossetti to come to the stage with the usual criticisms. Peter looked around as if dazed, then walked directly to the wings where the Costume Crew was standing. Everyone watched. The usual backstage hubbub fell to a silence as Peter walked up to Suzy who stood petrified, not guessing what could happen next.

Peter attempted a smile but it died immediately. He spoke as genially as he could, but his voice still shook with fury.

"You. Would you like to go to the Spring Dance with me?"

Melissa snickered. Suzy would never forgive her that snicker, although it was remarkable she heard it at all, for she felt any minute now she would faint. Here was one of those far-out, ridiculous daydreams coming true. Suzy gulped. Even in her confusion she realized the situation was disastrously wrong. It was clear that Peter was spiting Melissa by asking Suzy to go to the dance.

He waited, steel blue eyes never leaving hers.

"Yes. Thanks. I'll go with you," she said. Her voice had dropped its pitch so low, she wondered if anyone could have heard what she said, but she spoke in one of those rare moments when an un-explained silence makes the least sound magnify as though it were yelled through a high powered mike.

"Thank *you*, thank you very much," Peter said

formally, his eyes still burning with anger. Then he turned around to meet Melissa's apparently amused gaze as if to say, "There, see what I think of you! I'd rather go with what's-her-name than with you."

Melissa laughed a fake, theatrical ha-ha. As if she cared. . .

Peter began to walk away, then turned and came back to Suzy, this time less angry, to ask in a low voice, "By the way, what's your name?"

"Suzy. Suzanne Simmons," she whispered in a hoarse voice.

Mr. Rossetti was calling all the cast to the stage.

"Okay Suzy, I'll be seeing you," Peter said and left her.

Miss Pritchett called all the girls back to the Costume Room to finish a hundred dangling details, but first they crowded around Suzy.

"Hey, Suzy, Peter asked you! Are you going with him?"

"That's something. The Spring Dance is the big thing around here."

"Listen, Suzy, it's not one of the junior high dances with jukeboxes and jeans. This is for real. And you're going with Peter, a senior! Wow!"

"Are you ever lucky! I wish I were you."

"Well, I don't," Nan said firmly. "Melissa is really mad about this. She doesn't look it, but she is. Boy, better watch out, Suzy!"

Suddenly Suzy's knees gave way and she had to sit down. Her head was spinning — Peter, the dance, a new dress. Melissa dangerous? Was it real? Was it some daydream that had been confused with reality? She felt herself on a roller coaster slowly and inevitably rising up and up to its highest point, and then it would zoom down the other side and nothing would stop it.

"Help, let me off!" she wanted to cry.

Yet she wanted to stay. She was going to the Spring Dance with Peter, the great Peter Gilbert. What more could any girl ask?

Chapter 11

Overnight she changed from Suzy Nobody to Suzy Somebody. How the word traveled so quickly, she did not know. She had been careful to say nothing about it at home and she had even kept it from Patty and Mousie as they walked to school, because Suzy herself could not really believe it had happened, although she believed it did. In that case then, it was more than likely that today, the day of the opening, Peter would come to his senses and apologize to Suzy for having made such an invitation in the heat of anger and withdraw it. In that case, the fewer people who knew about it, the better.

But at school, even before classes began, two girls whom she did not know stared at her and whispered together. Three boys whistled to her as she walked into the school and a boy she did not know called out, "Hi, Suzy!" In the locker room at gym, two girls, juniors, who had dressed and undressed beside her since the beginning of the year, now spoke to her for the first time. These were girls whom Suzy had long wanted to know, girls who measured as high eights, possibly nines, on her grading chart.

"Say, are you Suzy Simmons?" Billie, the one with the red-gold hair and the heart-shaped face asked her.

"Yes, I am."

"Is it true that Peter Gilbert asked you to go to the Spring Dance last night, backstage, in front of everybody?" Terry, the tall, dark, thin one, asked.

"I guess so," Suzy mumbled.

"Well, congratulations!" Billie said and they both grinned at her. "That's news. Nobody ever thought he'd ever look at anyone but Melissa."

"You mean, he's never gone out with anybody else?"

Billie and Terry questioned each other with their eyes, then shook their heads. "Not as far as we know. How'd it happen?"

"Is it true that he and Melissa have been fighting at rehearsals?"

"I don't know that much about it," Suzy answered shyly. . .or slyly.

The gym teacher's impatient whistle saved her from having to explain as the girls rushed out to the gym floor. On the way, Billie asked Suzy to have lunch with them that day. "We eat in the North Grove, okay?"

"Terrific. Thanks. I'll meet you there," Suzy said. She was more overwhelmed than she wanted them to know. Lunch with Billie and Terry. Then she remembered, Terry was the editor of the school paper. Wow!

Yet all through gym class, random thoughts worried her. Possibly Billie and Terry weren't really interested in her, only curious about Peter; then again, maybe they could be interested. A more troublesome fear was that if Peter should take back his invitation now, she would be known as the girl that Peter turned down. Then what would Billie and Terry say?

Still another complication came of this later that morning, before lunch, when Mousie and Patty ran up to Suzy.

"Why didn't you tell us Peter asked you to the dance?" Mousie asked, her feelings hurt.

"It didn't seem important," Suzy lied, trying to spare Mousie's feelings.

"Let's have lunch and you can tell us about it," Patty said, obviously enthused about it. "I think that's *neat*, real neat."

And now Suzy would have to hurt them again. "I'm sorry, really, but I can't eat with you today."

"You can't! But you always eat with us," Patty said, her wide face troubled. Mousie, half understanding, pulled her away.

"It's all right, Suzanne Simmons, if that's how you want it," she said in a proud, hurt kind of way.

Suzy's mother would have said, there, this is a good opportunity to break with them, because they'll never do you any good at all. But Suzy couldn't bear the hurt in Patty's eyes and the disdainful shrug of Mousie's shoulder, because hypersensitive Mousie was also wounded.

"Hey, you two. Hold on. It's not that I don't want to be with you. I do. It's just that something else has come up. I can't see you after school either because tonight's the opening of *Oklahoma*. You're coming, aren't you? Can we get together tomorrow? You can come over to my house."

"Sure," Patty smiled, immediately forgiving.

Mousie remained injured longer, but Suzy poked her arm lightly and she brightened. "Okay, we'll see you tomorrow."

Lunch with Billie and Terry was something she promised herself she would always remember. The North Grove was part of a city park that adjoined the school. The trees above them were putting out the first hint of leaves, the sun was shining down warmly, and there Suzy sat with two girls she had long wished would be her friends.

For the most part Suzy listened and they talked. They appeared to know more about what was going on than she did, about the other members of the cast, the friendships and the breakups, and the judgments on which individuals would go professional.

"Well, Peter, of course. Someday Suzy, you'll be able to tell your children or grandchildren, you went out with the famous Peter G."

Suzy laughed. "I can't even think of myself being old, like that, getting married and having kids. Not for me, at least not for ages!"

"Melissa might make it. I'm not that sure about her."

"But I am," Terry disagreed. The two of them talked almost as though Suzy weren't there, passing opinions about Nell, the leading dancer, who would most definitely get into the American Ballet company, and what about Kim Chang, the cellist in the orchestra, fantastic Kim Chang!

Where have I been, Suzy wondered to herself. Here were all these remarkable people and she hadn't even noticed them. It was almost as if Peter alone filled her mind. But now Billie was confronting her.

"You're doing costumes. Are you into costumes? Do you design them or anything?" she asked eagerly.

"No. I just help out," Suzy mumbled modestly.

"Billie's into commercial art and I'm on the school paper," Terry explained quickly. "What about you?"

How she would give anything to mention casually that she was something of a concert pianist or that she made sculpture! Anything exotic.

"I like math a lot and I read a lot of science fiction," Suzy said, embarrassed because it sounded so common.

"That's wonderful," Terry said politely. "Are you in the Chess Club? Science Club?"

"Listen, with Peter taking her out," Billie said, "she's *okay*. She doesn't have to belong to any club."

"I was thinking that maybe she'd want to work on the school paper next year. We're going to need new faces. What about that?" Terry asked.

"Could be. Not now, but maybe later," Suzy said. She disliked writing, and yet if she were someone, if she belonged to something, then maybe she would have friends like Billie and Terry.

The bell rang. The girls cleaned up the remains of their lunch and wandered back across the grass to school. Was it possible that they really liked Suzy? She wondered and hoped it was so.

It was a strange day, a day in which Suzy's spirits bounced high and then fell to the ground again, a yo-yo day. In the restroom mirror she stared at herself. If only her hair would grow— could it grow three inches in two weeks, in time for the dance? Unlikely. If only she were taller. If only her figure were better. A tall girl, a senior with long, silky, swinging blond hair pushed in beside Suzy, smiled at herself in the mirror, and instantly Suzy was plunging down to Suzy Nobody again, a plain freshman girl with short brown hair, who wasn't tall enough.

If only she could understand why it was happening, that people she didn't even know said hello to her in the halls, even "Hi, Suzy!" and that two junior girls asked her to have lunch with them, and that Peter had not yet retracted his invitation. Why wasn't she happier then? For a moment she wished she were plain Suzy that nobody knew.

When she entered math class she saw a neat white envelope on her desk, her name written on it in precise square letters. Immediately she knew it had to be from Peter who was telling her the invitation was a mistake and would she forgive him, etc.

Slowly she opened the envelope and pulled out the note. A piece of paper neatly cut from a notebook was marked with one sentence in the same careful penmanship.

"Don't go to the Spring Dance with Peter."

What? Peter would not have written an odd note like that. She was sure of that. Then she remembered he wasn't in school that day, excused because of the opening that night. Besides, he wouldn't have known which classes Suzy had or where she sat.

She turned the paper over and found no clue as to who might have sent it. Melissa? She vaguely remembered someone telling her to watch out for Melissa's temper. Was this a threat or a piece of advice? She did not want to tangle with that Melissa, not for a minute, as she remembered the mean way in which she had stomped on Peter's toe with the heel of her boot and the way she had slapped his face.

Suzy sat ramrod straight in her seat, for the first time too preoccupied to pay attention to the problems Mr. Stone was setting up on the blackboard. For the first time she could not center her attention on geometry and, blushing, slid down in her seat while someone else solved the problem.

Mercifully she remembered a detail. The note could not have come from Melissa, for Suzy had been in the Costume Room when Melissa signed a paper saying she was using a shawl that had been loaned by Ms. Henry, and her handwriting had impressed Suzy because it was so large and some-how boisterous, the writing of an extrovert. She probably could not have imitated the small neat letters of the note, even if she'd wanted to.

No matter who sent it then, it upset Suzy considerably because her first reaction was to agree spinelessly, to say "All right, I won't go." Her second reaction welled from the depths as she argued with herself. "What, not go, when you've been dreaming of this for months and months?"

Then what should she do?

A stern, practical Suzy took over. She breathed

deeply, then laid the alternatives out in front of her.

First she would see what happened at the opening of *Oklahoma*. If Peter and Melissa made up, then he would most likely ask Suzy to forget the Spring Dance and she would answer him with grace, dignity, and understanding. No tears, no words of blame, no dramatics. And she would go on loving Peter secretly and alone, because he was the most magical person she had ever known or would know.

On the other hand. . .

If he said nothing, then she would go to the dance with him. The only complication she could foresee was that he might have forgotten all about asking her in the excitement of *Oklahoma*, and she would be dressed up and waiting and he would not show up.

But that was too far ahead, two weeks away, so she didn't have to worry about that yet. One step at a time!

In the meanwhile, she herself would say nothing about it. Nothing. Not a word. Thank heavens her parents didn't know.

That night, in honor of the opening of *Oklahoma*, Mrs. Simmons made chili beans and cornbread for dinner along with apple pie for dessert, all of which she prepared superbly and which Suzy loved. She could not eat for nervousness.

"Scared?" her father asked. "Butterflies in your tummy? First night shakes?"

"Sort of. I mean, last night one of the dancer's dresses fell off. What if that happens tonight? A million things can go wrong."

"Uh-uh," Cynthia said, picking up Marmaduke and rubbing her face in his mangled lion's fur. "Suzy's nervous because she's going to the Spring Dance with Peter Gilbert."

"With who? What Spring Dance?" Suzy's mother asked, her voice rising, as if she couldn't quite believe it.

"How did you find out, fink?" Suzy asked her sister in a low, menacing voice. Cynthia's school was located two miles in another direction. How *could* she have found out?

"Never mind," Cynthia said smugly. "I got spies. They tell me everything."

"Is this true, Suzy?" Dr. Simmons asked. "The Spring Dance is a senior dance, isn't it? Kind of a biggie? Who's the boy?"

"Peter Gilbert. Suzy's in love with him," Cynthia said.

Suzy reached across the table to slap her hand across Cynthia's mouth, but Dr. Simmons intervened.

"If you must know," Suzy said in a condescending way, only because she was unexpectedly close to tears of exasperation, "Peter Gilbert has the lead in *Oklahoma*. You'll see him tonight. He asked me to go with him last night, but I'm not sure if I will or not. I suppose one of Cynthia's cronies has a big nosy brother or sister in the cast."

Not acknowledging this, Cynthia went on. "What do you mean, you're not sure you'll go with him? You said yes last night, right in front of everyone. Everybody knows."

"Will you shut up? How do you get to know these things, you monster?"

"Now, Suzy, temper, temper!" Mrs. Simmons

said. "I can't understand why you look so unhappy. It sounds like a fairy tale, the lead of *Oklahoma* asking you to a dance. Are you sure that he did ask you?"

"MOTHER! Of course, I'm sure. You think I'm so ugly nobody would ask me? Is that what you think?"

"Suzy, take it easy," Dr. Simmons said.

"Well, Mother doesn't have to be so surprised. It's not as if I were the worst dog in school."

"I didn't say that. But it's possible that someone dared him to do it, or made a bet? It happens all the time."

"Mother, how can you go on and on like this?"

Suzy stood up, inadvertently knocking her silverware to the floor with a clatter. Cynthia smugly fished a piece of hamburger from the chili and fed it to Marmaduke. She grinned nastily at Suzy.

"Well, if I were a senior," Dr. Simmons said, "I'd sure ask Suzy to go to a dance with me. I think she's pretty cute."

"Thanks, Dad. I'd go with you too," Suzy said. "And now, I've got to get over to the school. I have to iron some costumes."

"You're not wearing jeans and that dreadful Save the Whales shirt, not on opening night, are you?"

"Work outfit. Backstage crew and all that. Can't take a chance of getting confused with some of the celebrities," Suzy said ironically, not wanting to be nasty to her mother and yet her mother seemed to be asking for it. She softened her tone of voice.

"Please, Mom and Dad, don't be late for *Oklahoma*. You'll want to see it from the beginning. I hope you like it."

"We will, pumpkin, we will. I'll be looking at those costumes. . ." Dr. Simmons said.

"And boasting to everyone in a loud voice that his daughter made them."

He probably will, Suzy thought, not knowing which was worse, a parent who could not believe you were capable of anything or one who brayed about the least thing you did.

"I'll die before this is all over," Suzy groaned, grabbing a jacket. She ran all the way to school, breathing in gulps of fresh, cool, evening air to calm her fevered spirit.

Chapter 12

Backstage, everything trembled with anticipation and nervousness. Suzy, ironing the dancers' calico skirts, paused to close her eyes and pray quickly. "Please, oh please, let it go well. Let it be perfect tonight. Let the play be terrific."

Possibly it was the force of everyone backstage praying in one fashion or another, or possibly it was the thoughts of the huge audience sending up hopes that all would go well, that *Oklahoma*, on its opening night, was a hugely successful production.

Miracles had happened. Those dancers who had been out with the flu recovered sufficiently to join the cast as if they'd never been away. The curtain did not refuse to budge while actors and actresses stood frozen on the stage as they waited for it to fall, something that had happened before. Nobody's costume fell off or ripped, at least not in obvious places. And the biggest miracle of all was that Peter and Melissa had never acted more beautifully, sung more sweetly, or performed with better spirit. Not an inkling of jealousy or meanness anywhere. This was how Curley and Laurie should be, in love with each other, eyes glistening and yearning.

"I love it. It's like magic. It gives me chills up and down my spine," Jan said as the Costume Crew watched from the wings.

"Like seeing it for the very first time," Nan said. Suzy could hardly believe it, the cynical Nan with tears in her eyes.

Suzy watched it, nearly crying herself because it was so beautiful after all. Or else tears threatened to come because Peter and Melissa were so perfect; how obvious it was that they belonged together. But she had always known that, hadn't she? All right, after the performance, much later that night, when Peter would come and explain why he couldn't take her to the dance, she would say, "It's all right, Peter. I understand." He would tell her how wonderful she was. Maybe he would kiss her before he left to find Melissa.

After the curtain calls—were there nine or ten? —as the crowd still cheered and the applause continued, the curtain closed for the last time. Backstage, it became a mob scene as the audience swarmed to congratulate the performers. Suzy, whose job it was to collect the costumes that were draped over chairs and fallen on the floor of the dressing rooms, to save them from being stepped on and ruined, was amazed to find herself seized and hugged and congratulated by her father, while her mother stood by and smiled happily. Suzy, embarrassed enough to faint, asked meekly if they liked it.

"Loved it! It was superb. And those costumes. . .

Mm," her father kissed his fingers, while Suzy reddened and hoped nobody saw him. "Anyone would have thought a French designer had made them."

"A beautiful production," Mrs. Simmons said, "and I'm saving the program because your name is on it. Did you see it?"

Suzy hoped nobody overheard. After all, she was only in the Costume Room.

"And I thought your Peter was magnificent. He is so talented!" Mrs. Simmons said and then lowered her voice to whisper. "Suzy, are you sure he asked you to the Spring Dance?"

This time Suzy lost her temper. "No, I'm not sure that he did. I probably just dreamed it up. And now, if you'll excuse me, honest, I've got to pick up all these costumes or they'll get ruined in this crowd."

"She's right. We mustn't interfere with her job," Dr. Simmons said. "We'll see you later. Suzy, want me to come and call for you when you're finished?"

"Thanks, but we're having a small cast party and Jan's father promised to take me home afterward. They live near us."

"Fine," he said. "See you later."

"Anyway, I'm proud of you, taking part in something fine like this," Mrs. Simmons said, giving Suzy a quick kiss. Suzy mumbled her thanks, for her mother could be very sweet at times. Yet she was relieved to see them go. And yet, she thought as she picked up three abandoned petticoats, it was nice that they had come backstage to see her.

The cast party, a loud victorious gathering, met in the multi-purpose room. Suzy guessed this was how soldiers must have felt when they'd won an important battle, relieved and happy. Mr. Rossetti was still wiping the perspiration from his face and combing back his nonexistent hair with his fingers. A small rock group who had been part of the orchestra now threw themselves into something far wilder than the score of *Oklahoma*, and the volume was so high, it was nearly impossible for one person to know what another was saying.

Suzy stood against the wall and watched.

Jan passed by her. "I guess Peter will be coming around to dance with you," she said arching her eyebrows. "This I gotta see. They're taking pictures of him now for the papers, but he'll be here soon."

Suzy hoped he would ask her to dance but hoped more that he wouldn't. The thought of getting out on a dance floor with such a performer was far too overpowering. She would stumble, she would get sick, she might faint! Almost immediately she prayed that he wouldn't ask her, not then.

Anyway, he's probably made up with Melissa, Suzy thought, fully expecting both of them to walk in together, in love as Peter and Melissa, just as they had acted the love of Curley and Laurie. And so Suzy was surprised when Melissa came in with an actor on either side; she danced first with one, and then with the other. Presently Peter walked in with two of the "cowboys." People crowded around him and he accepted compliments gracefully. Wherever he turned, a teacher or one of the lighting crew or someone was always there to stop and congratulate him or joke with him or tell him about the great future that lay before him.

But he did not ask Melissa or anyone to dance.

His eyes were brighter and his manner more radiant than Suzy could have imagined. He had tasted victory and loved it. Now he was a hero.

As if by accident, he caught sight of Suzy, signaled to her as if asking her to wait. He stopped long enough to pick up a glass of punch and walked over to her, practically shaking off his admirers.

This is it, Suzy was thinking, promising herself she would remain cool. But why did he have to choose a public place! Everyone would be watching.

"Here's a drink for you," Peter said, handing her the punch.

"Thanks." Suzy's voice sunk an octave. "Peter, you were wonderful tonight. A beautiful performance. Boy, are you great, really great!"

"So you liked it? You think it went okay?"

"It couldn't have been better."

"That's because the costumes were so good. By the way, Suzy, I love that wedding shirt you made."

"I didn't really make it. I just sewed on the buttons, but if they didn't pop off, then they were all right, I guess."

"They were tremendous," he said with gusto. The conversation was rapidly turning inane. Please, she prayed, let's get it over.

He hesitated. The blare of the band died down temporarily. To her relief he did not ask her to dance, but began to talk as soon as the music began again, a fast frenetic noise.

"Suzy, I have to ask you something. It's embarrassing."

"It's all right, I don't mind," she said coolly. It's coming now. She felt like one of her father's patients when he announced he was about to pull out a tooth.

"You're Suzy Simmons, I know that, but I haven't the foggiest about where you live. I think I can get a car the night of the dance and I'll call for you. But you'll have to tell me where."

So he was going through with it after all. Suzy was sure that Peter could hear her heart pounding audibly over the noise of the rock group.

"That's just wonderful, about borrowing the car, I mean," she said haltingly, then added, "I live at 17 Manzanita Drive. Do you know where it is?"

"I think so. I went to a party out that way once. I'll call for you at nine o'clock, something like that. All right?"

"Thank you."

"Think nothing of it." The conversation could have hardly become more minimal. "I'll see you then," he finished and walked back to his friends with the same exaggerated rolling cowboy gait he had used in the play.

So he had asked her to the dance and meant it. Now it was all right to be sure of it. Fireworks were bursting in her head so loudly that she could hardly hear Mr. Rossetti giving a speech of thanks, congratulations, encouragement, and orders to go home and get a good night's rest. Another performance faced them the next night.

Suddenly the room became too crowded and noisy. Forgetting all about her promise to wait for Jan's father to pick her up, Suzy rushed out into the night, welcoming its cool, quiet air. Soon she was running, running all the way home. Yet she lingered before going into the house.

Marmaduke was sitting on a fence, catlike and motionless. When he saw Suzy, he jumped down and came over to rub against her leg. Forgetting that this was her enemy, a killer of seven innocent birds, Suzy picked him up, held him in her arms and stroked the coarse, patchy fur. He purred.

Overhead the stars were out, millions of them, high and twinkling in a midnight sky. The Milky Way was spread out like a bridal veil.

"Twinkle, twinkle, little star. How I wonder what you are!" Suzy whispered to Marmaduke. A diamond in the sky? No wonder they called Peter the "star" of the show. He too was brilliant, shining, and yet remote, forever out of reach.

Chapter 13

Drifting. She was drifting through a strange, detached stretch of time that would not pass and yet leaped ahead. Soon *Oklahoma* would have seen its last performance and the following night she would be going to the Spring Dance.

Being Suzy Somebody did not mean a plunge into wild popularity, which was just as well, but at least she was no longer that anonymous unseen freshman that she was before. Billie and Terry asked her to join them at lunch several times and Terry kept hinting that Suzy should try out for the school paper even if she was a freshman. Even Jan and Lisa from the Costume Room invited Suzy to go to the yardage shop with them when they went shopping for material for summer clothes. People she did not even know smiled at her, and she was learning to smile back. It was pleasant to be Suzy Somebody at last.

But not entirely so. One afternoon as she was leaving school a roughly mannered boy and a girl with a blotchy skin and small ferrety eyes stopped Suzy, blocking her way.

"Hey, are you Suzy What'sit, the one Peter's takin' to the dance?"

The boy grinned rudely and the girl peered at Suzy so maliciously, that Suzy was taken aback. She knew she should tell them to go to the Devil or most likely something far cruder, yet she could not quite do that. Instead, she stood very straight, scanned them coldly with her eyes and walked away without a word. They stared after her and she hoped they felt cheated.

Yet something in their taunting expression upset her, as if they and possibly many others as well were waiting for her to take a pratfall. When she got up to recite in English class, she became haunted by the fear that she was being watched in just that way. It was worse than being on a stage, for there an actress impersonates someone else. Here she was playing her own role.

She had never thrown away the slip of paper that advised her not to go to the dance, but had thrust it into the bottom of her purse. Now and then, as she searched for a pencil or the ID card in the bottom of her wallet, she saw the note lying there. It made her furious, and yet she didn't throw it away.

Who were her real friends? Mousie and Patty. On the Saturday after the opening night of the play, Suzy, clad in a bikini, sat at the edge of Mousie's pool while Patty and Mousie, fully dressed, threw questions at her.

"I think it's wonderful," Patty said, her blue eyes glowing as if she were the one going to the dance. "Peter Gilbert, wow! What's he like?"

"Tell us, Suzy, how did it happen? What is he like, not the public image, everyone knows that, but when you're with him alone?"

"How come he's taking you to the dance?" Patty asked.

Suzy looked from Patty's eager face to Mousie's shiny, intent, hazel eyes, barely visible behind the dark glasses she liked to wear. These were her friends. If only she could tell them the truth, what a relief it would be! And yet it would only disappoint them.

"I — I don't really know what he's like."

"Of course you do. If someone asks you to an important thing like that. . ."

"Mousie, he didn't even know my name when he asked me."

"That's even more romantic," Patty cried. "He was in love with you secretly."

"Somehow, I don't see Peter as being that shy," Mousie said soberly.

"To tell you the truth, I don't know why he asked me," Suzy said, miserable now. She couldn't confess, not even to her good friends, that he had spoken to her exactly three times in his life and that he hardly knew her, let alone had romantic ideas about her.

"Are you in love with Peter? I'll bet you are. That's why you act so different. Here, have another brownie," Patty said, shoving a box of brownies she had made toward Suzy. Suzy began to take one, then put it back. These days she couldn't seem to eat.

"They look great but I have to fit in my evening gown," she smiled.

Patty took the brownie herself and nibbled at it while Mousie, whose policy it was never to eat anything that tasted good, sat with her thin legs pulled up and her chin resting on her bony knees as she squinted at Suzy.

"Why didn't you tell us about Peter before?" she asked.

"There was nothing to tell."

"Suzy, you just don't ask someone to go to the Spring Dance unless there's a reason. Like being in love. Or is there something about Melissa? I mean, I heard there was something funny going on. . . ."

"Look, you guys. I just don't want to talk about it," Suzy said, and with that she plunged into the pool and swam to the far side of it and back again. As she scrambled to the edge of the pool, she heard Patty talking about her almost as if she weren't there.

". . .he's in love with her, I think. After all, she's not bad looking, if only she'd let her hair grow. That ugly haircut, ugh!"

"Yes. YES, YES!" Mousie agreed.

"You know what's wrong with my haircut?" Suzy asked. "My mom makes me have it done with Marie down at the Hair-You-Are! And she wants me to have it trimmed before the dance. It's a real problem."

"Then fight!" Mousie cried. "Put your foot down. Tell her from now on you're the one who makes decisions about things that concern you."

Suzy hadn't dreamed Mousie had so much fight within her.

"You can be respectful. She *is* your mother after all," Patty said soberly, as if giving the matter deep thought. "Be respectful but firm. Say 'No, Mother,

I'm letting it grow. And I won't go to Marie's until I decide to do it!' "

Patty a fighter too? Suzy blinked. It was she who was the coward.

"She might be reasonable," Mousie continued. "Some of the time your mother is kinda neat."

"Then you should see her the rest of the time," Suzy said. It wasn't her mother that interested them, however. Never before had they seemed to care about her. No reason to begin now.

"All right," Suzy said. "I simply won't go to Marie's. I just won't go."

With that, a weight seemed to roll from her mind.

"What will you wear to the dance? Do you think he will send you flowers? Will you walk? Do you think he's gonna kiss you?"

They were flooding Suzy with questions. Patty wanted her to wear a pink dress, something with ruffles like the costumes in *Oklahoma*, and Suzy hesitated.

"Don't make me vomit," Mousie said. "They were terrif in the show, but not right for Suzy. Let's see, something off-white, not too fluffy, maybe something ethnic. Only slightly ethnic."

"I know," Patty cried excitedly. "She could wear something flowery and gauzy."

"Not flowery, but gauzy. Yes. Aha, I know just the thing. At the India Imports, an off-white dress, just a little embroidery, a chiffon scarf around your head. I'll let you take some gold bracelets. . ."

"And shoes. Not those clumpy things you're always wearing but sandals with tiny straps," Patty told her.

"You're getting me all excited," Suzy said. It

was exciting! She could never tell them the truth about Peter now, for she was touched that they seemed to care so much. They were doing so much for her, yet they couldn't help themselves. Well, she would help them someday, somehow.

One thing was certain now. She could not tell them the truth about Peter, especially if they had miraculously not heard about it already. On the night of the dance, Patty and Mousie would most likely be home alone, as she had all through junior high and nearly a whole year of high school. But they weren't jealous. In a way she was going for t!.em, representing them.

Someday, she promised, someday she would do something for them.

She fought with her mother about having her hair cut by Marie or anyone else.

"Are you crazy, Suzy? Long hair doesn't become you. It's out of style and besides you've always had short hair. At one time you listened to me."

"I did, did I?"

"Don't be fresh."

"I won't. But I'm not going. I've made up my mind about what I want."

Mrs. Simmons began to say something, then stopped shortly and sighed. "Nobody can say I haven't tried."

With that she gave in.

Neither Suzy nor Mrs. Simmons looked forward to shopping together one weekday after school. Yet it had to be faced.

It began timidly, each of them grimly determined to be pleasant.

"I wonder if you know what a dress is like.

You've been wearing jeans and shirts for so long, you've probably forgotten," Mrs. Simmons said. A great way to begin, Suzy mumbled as they entered the huge shopping mall just outside of Elmwood Heights. Mrs. Simmons was fingering some sweet flower-sprigged dresses with insets of lace.

"Mother, no. Not that!"

"All right. Something tailored then. A shirt and long skirt?"

"Yech!"

The afternoon pulled back and forth like a tug of war. Yet Suzy won. She found a long ivory cotton dress with the tiniest smattering of embroidered flowers on the bodice and sleeves, the very dress Mousie had in mind. When she came out of the fitting room, Mrs. Simmons nodded in slow, resigned agreement. Why, she was thinking, Suzy is growing up. She's almost pretty. And she loves that dress, even though it's awful.

"It's not what I would have chosen," Mrs. Simmons said, for it is not easy to give up the role of mother all at once, "but if you like it, we'll take it."

Suzy hugged her mother with a surprising show of gratitude, and immediately pulled back with some embarrassment at her spontaneous thanks.

"I guess there's just something about your first dance," Mrs. Simmons said with a slight tremor in her voice, as she paid for the dress.

At home that evening, Suzy experimented with new makeup, dressed in the new stockings and slender sandals with their high heels and tiny straps, and put on the dress. Happy now, she paraded before her mother and father.

"Is this my little girl growing up?" Dr. Simmons asked.

"Daddy, you're sentimental," Suzy said.

"About that makeup, I'll have to help you with it," Mrs. Simmons said. "But isn't there a performance of *Oklahoma* tonight?"

"I almost forgot," Suzy cried, dashing upstairs. Yet before changing to her jeans she lingered before the mirror. She was changing. A new Suzy was emerging, like a butterfly from a chrysalis.

It will be all right after all. "It will, it will, it will!" she said, as if promising the future. Then she took off the beautiful new clothes, and without removing the makeup, put on her old jeans and a shirt that had a picture of a Great Dane printed across the front. She cried good-bye to her parents and ran swiftly into the night.

Chapter 14

On the day of the dance Suzy felt herself by turns exhilarated and ill, so nervous she could not eat anything nor could she lie down and sleep it off. She walked to the library, tried to steady herself by beginning a new Ray Bradbury story, but could not get past the first page. The time of the day played odd tricks, sometimes crawling and then leaping ahead by hours.

She felt as if she were two individuals forever quarreling. At four o'clock she decided to call Peter and tell him she had the flu and couldn't go. At five minutes after four, she dialed half his phone number, and then another Suzy put down the receiver and walked to the closet where she ran her hand over the soft folds of the new dress. Of course she would go.

"You have to take chances in life to get anywhere," the brave Suzy said.

"Over my dead body," said the realistic Suzy.

Nevertheless, she bathed in a long, fragrant bath with bubbles that filled the bathroom with the scent of lavender. She examined herself in the long mirror after getting out of the tub; she would lose five pounds anyway, maybe ten. Had her hair grown? A little, enough so that it appeared shaggy. Half closing her eyes she saw it four inches longer, brown and shining. But it wouldn't grow before nine that night, not in two hours.

Slowly, deliberately, she powdered herself everywhere, sending up a small violet cloud around herself, then dressed slowly, wearing the best underwear she had — the peach lace panties and bra an aunt had sent her on her birthday, the white rustling slip that had to be worn under the gauze dress, the sheer stockings, the sandals with their slender shrimp-colored straps that were so unlike the thick heavy ripple-soled shoes she wore the rest of the time.

Then she leaned forward to apply makeup to a face that had almost never worn any. Her mother had taught her well. First she applied a creamy moisturizer, thinking of herself as a girl in a TV commercial. She rubbed in violet eye shadow, applied the blusher which made her glow — ah, she loved that — and finally the lipgloss. A good dousing of "Charlie," one of her mother's perfumes. Finally she put on the dress, that lovely dress with its soft ivory pleats and an occasional modest blossom embroidered here and there on the skirt. A careful brushing of her newly shampooed hair gave it a soft fluffiness, a kind of brown halo around her head.

"Suzy, is that you?" she asked the vision in the mirror. "Really you?"

Everything will go all right, she assured herself. She didn't look bad at all. Why, then, did she feel so tense? Why did she become so dizzy that she had to lie down on the bed and breathe deeply in order to keep. . .keep alive?

Downstairs her father worked in his studio and her mother was in the kitchen preparing plates of cheese, olives, crackers, and other good nibbles, presumably for company. Suzy stood in the kitchen door and watched until her mother turned and saw her.

"There you are! Terrific, Suzy! Turn around, let me see."

Suzy modeled for her mother, turning around slowly.

"Harvey, come here!" Mrs. Simmons called. Dr. Simmons grumbled, then came in from his studio with wood shavings mingling with his thick brown hair. On seeing Suzy, he burst into a beautiful smile.

"Well, look at her, look at her! My goodness, you're all grown up. Princess, you're a beauty."

"Oh, Daddy, really now, really!" Yet she was pleased.

"It's true, the absolute truth. Let's see, Evelyn, don't we have a little something for Suzy?"

"We certainly do," Mrs. Simmons said, giving Suzy a small white jeweler's box. Suzy, delighted, opened it and found two clip-on earrings — simple, yet lovely, rings of gold wire.

"Ooooh! Oh, Oh, Oh! I love them!"

She slipped them on, hugged her father and mother, and ran to admire the new earrings in the mirror. Yet she almost wished they hadn't bought this gift which she loved so much, for she felt guilty, as though she were going under false pretenses. Isn't it weird to go to a dance with a boy who has spoken to you three times in your life, she asked herself, each time little more than a few words. And yet Peter had asked her to go.

"Do you like them? I'm glad," Mrs. Simmons said. "Now then, Suzy, I think we should have a little talk."

Suzy did not dare protest as Mrs. Simmons led her to the white sofa in the living room while Dr. Simmons escaped, ducking into his studio.

"Now darling," Mrs. Simmons said in a confidential voice while Suzy wanted to flee. Heavens, I hope she isn't going to tell me the facts of life and all that, not NOW, Suzy was thinking. Nothing seemed more unnatural to her than this mother-and-daughter chat on the living room sofa.

"We've never met Peter. We don't know much about him personally. Of course we know he's charming, handsome, and a very good performer. But we don't know how he might behave personally. I hope he won't take advantage of you."

"Mo-therrrrr!" Suzy protested.

"Hold on, Suzy. I'm saying this because even the nicest boys sometimes try to see how far they can go. Now many girls, even young girls, go much too far, you know what I mean. But I'm going to trust you, Suzy. Do you know how to say no?"

Suzy grunted. "This is the most sickening conversation. . ."

"Just remember, tonight may be glorious but there's always tomorrow," her mother said.

"For heaven's sake, Mother, I can't stand this conversation. It's so embarrassing."

"You can be embarrassed worse than this," Mrs. Simmons said. "I'll let you go, but don't forget our little chat, will you?"

"I'll remember it to my dying day, which may be tomorrow," Suzy said, wondering why she was so nasty when her mother meant well.

She got up, skirting a new green fern in the atrium, which came down too low so that it was necessary to duck while walking by it. She nearly bumped into Cynthia who was walking into the kitchen with Marmaduke in her arms. He was straining as if he would dearly like to leave, but Cynthia held on. Maybe that was Marmaduke's problem! A new insight, but this was not the time for it.

"Who's company, Mom?" Cynthia asked, swiping a delectable canape for herself. She offered the dish to Suzy who took one look at the fancy rounds of toast covered with mushrooms, shrimp, and olives and thought she would throw up. Not that she wouldn't adore that canape there with the anchovy, but not now, not now.

"The Burgers are coming over for a game of bridge, and they asked specifically if they could come early and see Suzy before she goes off to the dance."

"No, no, NO!" Suzy shrieked. "Mom, do they have to come. You didn't say yes, did you?"

"What's the matter with you? Of course I said yes. They love you, Suzy, they really do. They think there's nothing more wonderful than daughters..."

"No wonder, with their three rotten sons," Suzy said.

"Don't be mean. Let them enjoy you a little."

"But, Mother, Peter will be coming here."

"They won't chase him away."

Suzy groaned. For once, Cynthia was sympathetic. She even squeezed Suzy's hand in understanding. Charlie Burger (whom they called a Charlie burger with a pickle on a sesame seed bun) and Helen Burger (A Helenburger with catsup, please!) were the dullest, meatiest looking people either Suzy or Cynthia had ever met.

"I don't really have anything against them," Suzy said weakly. "It's just that tonight is so special . . ."

"Then share it. Be kind. Share it," Mrs. Simmons said.

Her mother was invincible.

Suzy trudged upstairs, opened the Bradbury but still couldn't get into it, and threw herself across the bed and buried her face. What did she want?

More than anything else in the world, at that point she found herself wishing she had a splendid, intelligent dog who adored her, her dog, and that the two of them were hiking over fields and past the woods as far away from Elmwood Heights as they could get.

The next minute she raised her head. Was she weird, wishing something like that when any time now, she would be going out with Peter? What was wrong with her?

The doorbell sounded its coy "Tea for Two" message and she jumped up trembling, then collapsed in a chair. It was only the Burgers. She could hear the Charlieburger's hearty grumphy laugh and the Helenburger's tittering mewing high-pitched giggle.

"Will you come down, dear, and let us see you?" Mrs. Simmons called.

Suzy, safe in her room, made a gurgling idiot face, then becoming Sweet Suzanne, walked down, smiled at the Burgers, turned around so they could admire her dress, made polite noises, and answered their endless questions about *Oklahoma*, all of them quantitative. How many in the cast, how many costumes, how many in the lighting crew, where did the prop director find that wonderful surrey. And so on. What bores, what bores, what endless bores they were! Eventually she got away, escaping to her room.

It was nearly nine. She fidgeted, had to remember to stop biting her nails, something she hadn't done since she was five years old. The polite voices of the Simmonses and the Burgers floated upstairs and Suzy swore that when she grew up she would not be like them.

Suddenly there was a scuffle in the atrium, the sound of leaves, a pot crashing and her father's voice, subdued but intense.

"That Damcat. Cynthia, come here. That cat is to stay outdoors at all times."

Cynthia's high voice, pitiful for the occasion: "But Daddy, he's not feeling well. And he's my little kitty..."

Suzy prayed. Please, keep Marmaduke out of the way when Peter comes. What would Peter think of them if Marmaduke acted up again!

Nine o'clock had passed, for it was now five minutes after the hour. Cynthia, without Marmaduke, burst into the bedroom. "It's late. Maybe he won't come."

"So what?" Suzy said. The same fear had occurred to her. "Your cat stinks."

Cynthia stuck out her tongue and vanished. Suzy paced the floor. A car door slammed on the street below and Suzy stood breathless, ready to answer the door when it rang, but the bell remained silent. It was now nine fifteen.

What was the etiquette of being stood up? Suzy knew nothing about it, and asked herself questions. How long does one wait? When do you give up and jump out of the window?

She adjusted her earrings, put on more eye shadow, borrowed her mother's mascara (although her mother said it was far too old for her), and stood at the end of the hall where she could see all the cars that passed. A large geranium stood in a pot. She plucked a leaf from it, then another leaf, hardly knowing what she was doing until she saw she had nearly stripped it and the leaves lay over the floor. Her mother would kill her.

It grew suspiciously quiet downstairs, tense, as if her parents and the Burgers too were sitting on the edge of their seats.

"Maybe they're holding a prayer meeting for me, concentrating on Peter," Suzy thought, groaning aloud at the thought.

At nine thirty she gave up, sat before her lavender desk and decided it was time to get undressed and crawl quietly into bed and never get out again.

At precisely nine thirty two, the doorbell rang. She jumped up as though an electric current had gone through her. Mrs. Simmons whispered loudly from the bottom of the stairs. "Suzy, he's here. Want to open the door?"

"In a minute," Suzy called languidly.

Assuming a pose that bordered on indifference, she "floated" down the stairs and opened the door.

There he stood. Peter, beautiful Peter, Peter in white blazer, shirt, and the purest and sharpest of tailored white pants she had ever seen. A White Knight.

"Hi, Suzy. Ready?"

His voice still excited her, now as on that very first day when he had knocked her down and spoken to her in the hall. "I hope I'm not late."

"I hadn't noticed," she said. She would have forgiven him anything, he was so radiant, so princely.

"Aren't you going to ask Peter in?" her mother called out with an artificial sweetness to her voice that drove Suzy to distraction.

"Do you want to come in? You don't have to," she whispered, but Peter stepped forward and then she had to introduce him. He smiled, shook hands with all four grinning adults, and charmed them with his manners. Suzy was wishing they could leave when Cynthia wormed her way between Suzy and Peter, her small round stomach pressed out and long pale hair prettily tousled.

"Don't forget me. I'm Cynthia, Suzy's young sister."

I'll kill her, Suzy thought.

"Well, hello, how are you?" Peter said, putting on his winning smile as though Cynthia were the most enchanting human being he had ever seen. Of course he had smiled at her parents and the Burgers in just the same way.

While Dr. and Mrs. Simmons threw shovelfuls of praise on Peter for his performance in *Oklahoma*, Suzy ran upstairs to snatch the mohair scarf her mother had let her borrow, warning her to put it away in her locker so it wouldn't get stolen. One last glance at herself in the mirror.

"Smile, Suzy, smile, smile, smile!"

She forced a wide, plastic, not entirely convincing smile and flew downstairs. Her father was talking with Peter at the door.

"Well, young man, how are you getting to the dance? Walking, bicycle, skateboard?" Her father was making little jokes. Suzy covered her ears. She would die before they ever left the house.

"Actually, I have a car."

And now, Suzy wondered, would her father ask to see his driver's license? Fortunately, he must have forgotten.

"Our Suzy is precious to us, you know, very precious. And this is her first dance. So bring her home by twelve. Think you can manage that?"

Suzy's cheeks burned. How could her father do this to her?

"Yes, sir, I certainly will, if you say so," Peter said agreeably.

"But Dad, we're just getting started at twelve," Suzy said.

Peter laughed a low charming laugh and immediately offered to shake hands with Dr. Simmons. He explained he'd love to stay and talk with him but it was getting late and they wanted to get to the dance.

"Good-*bye*!" Suzy said at last, going through the door as Peter held it open.

There seemed to be nothing to say as they walked through the serpentine garden path to the street, and then Suzy saw the car, a small, ancient MG. The side was bashed in where it had once met a larger and stronger force, but still the car had a rakish verve about it.

"What a dear, darling, little car! Wherever did you get it?"

"Borrowed it. Unfortunately it sometimes dies, particularly in the middle of traffic, but I ordered it to behave tonight."

Suzy laughed appropriately, but it sounded more as if a fish bone were stuck in her throat than a lighthearted appreciation of Peter's humor.

"The catch on your door doesn't work, Suzy, and it flies open when I go around corners, so if you don't mind just holding it closed until we get there. . ."

Her arms would fall off before they reached the gym, but she smiled agreeably. "I don't mind at all," she said as she grasped the handle.

Peter stepped into the car, sat behind the wheel, and after five minutes of coughing, gagging, and general protest, the car agreed to start and at last they were off to the dance.

Chapter 15

The big question was this: What would they talk about? Suzy hung onto the door handle as Peter swung around corners on two wheels, but in between the corners, a silence filled the air. Of course, they could talk about *Oklahoma* but he had been praised so much. Could he stand any more of it?

"It sure was terrific, wasn't it?" Suzy asked. "You were so fantastic, but I guess I've told you that and everyone thinks so. . . ."

Peter made a deprecating gesture, a show of pretended modesty.

"The reviews were fabulous. All raves," Suzy said.

"All except the review in the E.H. SHOPPING NEWS. That stunk."

"Oh well, who reads that?" Suzy said. The shopping news, a small advertising sheet delivered free and unasked, carried with it a page of local news and reviews. "Do you know who wrote that review? Sumner Barker. He's bright but he hates everything he sees. He's only twelve years old."

"He writes like a backward ten-year-old," Peter said sourly.

Suzy laughed and did not mention that Daniel Bright had once said Sumner was the only intelligent critic in town.

Peter drove around the high school parking lot and found a place in the farthest and darkest corner; a perfect spot for a kiss. Suzy held her breath; would he kiss her? If he did, what would she do? However, he didn't kiss her but jumped out and went around to open the door for her, a gallant gesture made useless because she had already opened it herself and jumped out. He could have put his hand on her shoulder or something, she thought, but instead he took out a comb, ran it through his hair, and grinned.

"We might as well get in and get it over with. Okay, Suzy?"

"Sure. I guess so."

That conversation died almost as soon as it had begun. Two feet apart, eyes straight ahead, they walked toward the gym from which the beat of a fast dance emanated into the parking lot. The gym had been darkened, but bright spotlights moved randomly around the hall so that now a green face emerged, there a blue profile, and somewhere else for a moment a bright orange hand appeared and became lost in the darkness again. Peter's eyes roved over the crowd as they stood in the doorway. After a brief pause, the band struck up a slow beat. Reluctantly Peter moved closer to Suzy.

"Shall we dance?"

"Sure, if you want to," she said.

If that solved the crisis of a dying conversation, a new problem took its place. Peter was much taller than she, or else she was shorter than she realized. As he took her in his arms, her face became buried in his shoulder. At least he could not see it burning helplessly with shame as he cut several intricate steps which she could not possibly manage. At one point she became entangled in his long elegant legs.

"Sorry," he said nobly, going back to a simple two-step that she was able to follow. He hummed with the music and it was clear he was bored.

Dances don't last forever. When the lights turned on and everyone applauded, Suzy realized she was still wearing her mother's mohair shawl, which suddenly become the most disgusting object she'd ever seen. She would have liked to drop it and let it get lost, but she had promised her mother she'd put it in her locker.

"Do you mind if I put this thing in my locker? My mother, you know. . ."

"Of course, perfectly all right," he said, his eyes already roving around the ballroom.

A locker in a corridor is hardly romantic, she thought, stuffing what she now considered a loathsome object inside and locking the door. Briefly she recalled old movies about balls held in Southern plantations where wraps were whisked away by convenient servants so no one ever had to worry about such things. She walked back to the dance floor slowly, wondering how long the dance would last.

The lights were on in the gym and the floor was frantic with a fast dance, girls in one line and boys in another. Peter was dancing opposite a girl named Stacey who had danced in *Oklahoma*, a girl with long black hair. She kept up with Peter well, and he came to life, dancing as though he were performing a solo on stage, turning, dipping, kicking, swaying, and always doing it in an unexpected way. A small crowd gathered around him and although Stacey was remarkably good, Suzy thought, still Peter was the center of the crowd, getting applause as he performed one amazing feat after another. Suzy's feet were tapping. She almost forgot her self-consciousness as she applauded Peter, but once the music stopped, she froze with fear.

"Maybe he'll just forget me," she hoped.

He was grinning, catching his breath and acknowledging his admirers, but then, as another fast dance began, he walked over to Suzy, a forced smile on his face.

"Well, hello. Shall we try again?" he asked.

"Could we just dance in the corner?" she asked timidly.

"If you like," he said gallantly, leading her to a far corner of the gym. This time he danced less vigorously (so as not to make her feel inadequate?) and making herself smile, she moved in time to the music. At one point, when she was beginning to relax and move more vigorously and freely, her shrimp sandals with their three-inch heels betrayed her and she staggered awkwardly in an attempt not to fall. Had anyone ever been more awkward, more gauche, more. . .the word came before she could stop it. . .miserable!

"Don't worry," Peter whispered as he danced close to her and moved away again. It must be awful for him, Suzy thought.

Another slow dance began. This time Peter sang along with the music. If Suzy wanted to see him, she had to strain her neck. Otherwise she stared into his shoulder. Yet when she did glance up, she saw that Peter's eyes were roaming around the gym, winking now and then at someone, she didn't know who. Possibly he was signaling for help. And it was still so early in the evening! Suzy remembered a movie she had seen where a man, stuck with a girl on the dance floor, held out a five-dollar bill behind her back to anyone who would cut in. She wondered, was Peter doing that?

The dance had hardly ended, however, when a flurry of excitement arose. A bright spotlight settled on Melissa, followed by Al Sakovich, who had just entered. Immediately the band broke into a wild version of *Oklahoma* and the crowd broke into whistles, cheers, and applause.

"Wow! Is she ever beautiful tonight!" someone yelled loudly.

True. Standing and smiling like a movie star, with long blond hair tumbling over a shimmering white dress cut remarkably low in front, far from the sweet calicos and muslins of the musical, Melissa waved her hand to the audience as if she were a queen greeting her subjects.

Peter had been holding Suzy's hand but at the sight of Melissa, he let it drop. He neither applauded nor cheered, but his eyes did not leave her for a second. At last Suzy had to face the truth. Peter was in love with Melissa and had been all along. Only a man in love could have such yearning in his eyes.

It would have been so much kinder if only he had

withdrawn his invitation! It would have hurt at first, but she would have recovered. She supposed he was being a good sport then and he was being a good sport now. How she hated good sportsmanship, if that's what it was!

Suzy applauded politely along with everyone else but wondered how she would get through the evening which stretched out before her for hours and hours. A sickly smile parted her lips while she prayed for escapes, a trapdoor that would open in the floor so that she could fall through, crawl through the space below the floor and go home. What about a spaceship that would swoop down and carry her off to Alpha Centauri or any other place? A masked stranger could burst through the door and carry her off. Then again, she might simply fall dead, a definitive escape.

Nothing happened. She was condemned to plod on through the evening. She could not tell which was worse, the many fast dances or the slow. While a hundred boys clustered around Melissa, Peter, his smile increasingly grimmer, danced every dance with Suzy.

"It's all right if you want to dance with someone else," she said after a long and particularly frantic scramble.

"Not at all," he replied gallantly, beginning another dance. His eyes followed every movement of Melissa's.

"How about some punch?" he asked, leading Suzy to the reception room where one of the teachers, acting as chaperone, served them both.

Fortunately Suzy didn't have to worry about conversation, because any number of friends slapped him on the back, kidded him while he answered cleverly enough, and insisted on chatting with him.

"Hey Curley, what happened to the curls?"

"Petah, you're marvelous. Absolutely!" This was from a girl with a British accent, probably fake, someone Suzy had never seen before. Suzy hung back, sipping her punch slowly, as if she didn't belong to Peter and he didn't introduce her to anyone.

Someone called out rudely, "Hey, Gilbert, you want to get Melissa back? You'll have to fight Sakovich. Got your insurance paid up?"

Peter threw his head back and laughed falsely and charmingly. More people joked with him and Suzy stood by dumbly, feeling like a little sister who had been dragged along.

"Shall we try again?" Peter asked gamely, a frustrated yet noble smile on his face.

After the torture of three fast dances and a slow one, Suzy excused herself to go fix her makeup. The girls' room was crowded with girls, half of them chattering loudly and most of them putting on fresh makeup and loving themselves in the mirror. Two sad girls stood in the corner and watched. Suzy lingered too.

When the room was fairly clear, one girl explained. "My mother made me go and I haven't danced once tonight. I knew it would happen."

"It's not the worst thing that can happen to you," Suzy said.

"Look who's talkin'. You came with Peter, dincha?"

Then they saw the misery in her eyes. But she'd better do something or she'd become a loser, like those girls. Leaning over the basin, she plastered on more blusher, eye shadow, and lipgloss, nearly satisfied with the way she looked, when four pretty girls burst into the room, talking fast and loud and bursting into laughter. Even when they were in the booths, they went on talking, then came out to wash their hands, smile at themselves in the mirror, and then flounce out again, not even noticing the three girls who watched them the whole time.

"It's so easy for them," one of the girls said.

When Suzy returned to the battleground, the lights were dimmed and a spotlight centered on Peter and Melissa who danced a slow dance perfectly and professionally, as though it were a stage performance.

What a beautiful story it would be, Suzy was thinking, if only she weren't the butt of it. Should she go to the locker, take her mother's shawl, and disappear? She could walk around until midnight, then walk home and rave about the wonderful time she'd had. But Peter might miss her, and then possibly someone would go out to find her and it would be embarrassing. Things were bad enough now but she'd never live that down.

Besides, the dance ended and even as people applauded, Peter recognized her standing against the wall and nodded to her. She was feeling almost as sorry for him as for herself. They were both stuck. Yet he smiled wanly as he approached.

"I was afraid you'd walked out on me. You wouldn't do that, would you, Suzy?"

"Of course not," she said, realizing for the first time how mortified he would be if that unknown freshman walked out on him.

"I love what they're playing," he said, actually

much brighter and livelier than he was when they first came. "Come on, Suzy. Let's try it. It's easy. Honest, it is."

As they danced, he whispered in her ear. "You know, this is a pretty dull affair, so some of us are going over to Fountain Blue. You know where it is, don't you?"

"Sure."

"There's a great trio playing there tonight, Bud Landon. Really cool stuff. Some of us thought we'd leave after the next dance. What do you think, Suzy? It's up to you."

"Why, sure, anything is all right with me," Suzy answered, feeling far too spineless. Afterward, if Peter remembered her at all, he would probably think of her as the girl that was like a dish of cold mashed potatoes. All that Suzy really wanted was to go home.

However, at the appointed time, eight couples congregated outside the door. The fresh air and dark night revived Suzy temporarily. She glanced up at the stars and they winked at her. Nothing lasts forever, they seemed to say.

Once more she sat beside Peter and held on to the door while he sang loudly and brought the MG up to maximum speed as he curved around the car in which Melissa sat beside Al. How fortunate, Suzy thought, that her father didn't know about that!

Fountain Blue was an improvement over the gym because it was so dark and packed with people, that she was able to feel anonymous. The Bud Landon trio in the small redwood gallery above the ice cream parlor played with maximum power, making conversation impossible. The couples managed to slip into two booths where they were jammed in closely. Peter and Al brought over frozen yogurts for everyone, but within minutes, as if they couldn't wait, Peter and Melissa were bobbing up and down on the tiny dance floor in back. The others seemed to disappear too, so that Suzy found herself sitting beside Al Sakovich. She had never realized how big he was; she felt tinier than ever. He reminded her of the giant in "Jack and the Beanstalk," but he wasn't mean in the least. Rather friendly in fact. He ate his double helping of frozen fudge yogurt, then tapped on the table with his spoon to the beat of the music.

"You don' wanna dance, do you?" he asked.

"No, thanks anyway. I'd just as soon listen."

"Me, too. You're kinda nice. What's your name?"

"Suzy. Of course I know who you are. Everyone knows."

"No kiddin'! Didja go to the games?"

"Just one. You were terrific," she said, hoping he would not ask which one, for Elmwood Heights High had suffered a dreadful defeat that time.

Did time pass slowly or quickly? A matter of relativity, Suzy decided, and tonight was an eternity. At least Al was surprisingly comfortable. He kept offering to buy her another frozen yogurt and when she thanked him but showed him she couldn't even finish the first, he did not press her. They sat and waited.

"Great music, isn't it?" he asked.

"Terrific," she lied. What a coward! She wondered if Al was as miserable as she was.

When the Landon group took a break, the room still seemed to shake. Peter, Melissa, and the others, now breathless, crowded back into the booths, joking and joshing one another. Peter slid in the booth and sat beside Suzy. In some ways he appeared much happier than before.

"I should've asked you to dance first, but you didn't really want to, did you, Suzy?"

"No, but that's okay. I understand."

"You're a very sweet kid. You really are."

It was a compliment that brought her close to tears. Being a good sport was cold comfort. He put his hand over hers.

Landon returned and stood up. A drum roll begged for quiet.

"We've had a request. It's not what we usually play but someone wants it and here it is! 'Where Do We Go from Here?' "

A cheer broke out.

"Suzy, let's try this one. It's easy, not too fast, not too slow."

"Well, if you like."

She noticed too that Melissa and Al were getting up to dance and she wondered if Melissa and Peter had arranged this. In its way, it was kind of them. This time something happened. The dancing became easier. Peter held Suzy close enough and guided her. She closed her eyes and let the dance happen. How easy it was after all! How well it was going!

"Not bad! Much better!" Peter said as the soft chords died away. He walked with her through the crowds back to the booth, but before he got there the trio embarked on a fast frenetic piece and he left her to dance with Melissa.

Again she sat beside Al and toyed with her yogurt. She yawned. After another dance — she was losing count — Peter returned.

"Hey, Suzy, do you know what time it is? I've

got to get you home by twelve or your old man's gonna be after me with a shotgun. I'm sorry to break this up, but he did ask me."

"That's all right. That's fine," Suzy said, getting up, and saying good night to everyone. Al smiled at her and said it was real nice knowing her.

The car would not start. "Come on, baby!" Peter begged and kicked it. It started and Peter, humming something or other, drove her home. At the door he kissed her quickly on the cheek, then rang the bell. When Dr. Simmons opened the door, Peter said cheerfully, "Here's your daughter, Dr. Simmons, safe and unharmed. It was wonderful being with her. Good night, Suzy, and thanks for a terrific time."

He spoke too loudly, Suzy thought, probably for the benefit of her parents and the Burgers who would be listening. Dr. Simmons blundered again but Suzy was too miserable to care.

"When I said midnight, of course I meant when the dance was over, something more like one, but that's all right, son. Thanks a lot, young man."

"Goodnight," Suzy said softly to Peter.

The Burgers were still there, still sitting in the Eames chairs as if they hadn't moved all night. A last spurt of courage held Suzy together.

"Did you have a good time, dear?" Mrs. Simmons asked. Everyone leaned forward to listen.

"A *good* time? It was marvelous, yummy, super, fantastic, beautiful!"

Any more and her voice would have quavered with hysteria.

"My feet are killing me, so I guess I'll go up," she said. "Good night."

Grinning widely to convince them, she lingered

just long enough so they wouldn't think she was on the verge of tears. Then she rushed upstairs, locked herself in her room, threw herself on the lavender bed, and at last indulged the long awaited relief of stifled sobs.

Chapter 16

She wept. In fact she could do nothing else at the moment but sob into her pillow, aware that her parents must not hear her, for then they would rush in to comfort her. It would be best to pretend she was asleep. She undressed quickly, letting her beautiful clothes fall to the floor in a pitiful heap. She turned out the lights and crawled under the covers. With luck she would lie there forever.

Yes, she wanted to die. The evening had been a nightmare, the Grand Jilt. Peter was lost forever. Never again would she be able to daydream about him. Even now he and Melissa were probably dancing at Fountain Blue or out riding in Peter's car. She hoped Melissa's arm would break off as she held the door.

And it was all her fault. She knew, really knew that Peter and Melissa went together and she was an outsider, but she didn't want to believe it. Why hadn't she paid attention to that neat warning note that told her not to go? Why hadn't she followed her own instincts which so wisely told her to call it off? Because she was in love with Peter, and even now he was as distant as a star in the sky.

Yet, everything considered, Peter had been kind, noble. Mistaken, but noble. He had gone through with what had to be an ordeal for him. Toward the end it had been almost wonderful, dancing together, as if at last she were catching on. At that point she could have danced until the next morning. But he had kissed her on the cheek as if it were a duty. He had called her "a sweet kid." Sweet kid! As if she were someone's little sister.

"Oh, God," she groaned, "let me die."

The worst part was that now everyone would know what had happened, that Peter had dropped her fast. Being Suzy Nobody now seemed an ideal state, for in the last few hours she had sunk to becoming Suzy Less-Than-Nobody. How could she possibly go back to school on Monday! She fell asleep and dreamed of faces leering and jeering at her while Peter and Melissa waltzed off into the sunset.

She woke at six thirty in the morning and this time she did not feel grief half so much as a gnawing inner emptiness. On further analysis, she decided it was not psychic but physical. She was hungry. In fact, starving. After all, she had eaten almost nothing during the past few days.

Her face felt filthy, greasy, smeared. Disgusted, she creamed her face, wiped off the makeup left over from the night before, and then scrubbed her face with a lufa sponge and soap until it felt clean once more. Then she picked up the lovely, gauzy dress from the floor, half apologizing to it for her carelessness. She held it close to her cheek and tears filled her eyes. They drifted down her face as she hung the dress carefully on a padded hanger and put it away in her closet. Poor dress, to have been worn once and possibly never again.

More tears. This would be one of those dreadful days when she would weep if someone wiggled a finger at her. Her parents would be sure to ask a thousand questions, how was the dance, what is Peter like, how many boys did you dance with, and so on, mercilessly. She had carried it off all right the night before, but today she would weep, for she was a failure as a liar, completely unconvincing, and the truth would bring on a river of tears. Then her father would say, "All right, Suzy, little girl. Get it off your chest. Tell Papa all about it."

Impossible. Now that she was in high school, she still loved her parents but no longer wanted to be "their little girl." If only she could escape somewhere.

Her stomach rumbled. First things first then! Putting on robe and slippers and recovering sufficiently to grab the new Ray Bradbury, she tiptoed down to the kitchen to make breakfast. On Sundays in the Simmons house, everyone was allowed to sleep late and take a private breakfast or wait for one of Mrs. Simmons' delicious brunches, usually featuring blueberry pancakes and sour cream. This was one of the few reasonable rules in the Simmons household.

Suzy put up two cups of coffee (forbidden) for herself and beat an egg for an omelet. On second thought she added another egg to the mixture, grated some Swiss cheese, made toast and spread the Bradbury novel in front of her. This condemned prisoner would eat a hearty breakfast. Yet even as she spread raspberry jam on her toast, tears started up in her eyes again. Even the first sip of fragrant coffee could not comfort lost love. She remembered how beautiful Peter had looked, how elegantly he had danced, how pure and blue were his eyes. Prince Charming.

If only she hadn't tested reality and gone to the dance, then she could build fantasy on fantasy and nobody would ever know. Maybe that was love, weaving daydreams, not trying to experience them. Now she had lost Peter. The Prince was gone forever. She told herself sternly she would never fall in love again. Never.

She consoled herself with an extra spoonful of jam.

Something warm, furry, and comforting rubbed against her leg. Well, it was Marmaduke himself, playing friends as he gazed at her and mewed softly. He placed his ginger paws on her knees and mewed again, almost as if he were comforting her. Was he asking to be loved or was this a trick from the archenemy, the killer of parakeets? A tear fell from Suzy's cheek to the top of his nose, and he lapped it up, his gaze never leaving hers. And so she picked him up and he was content to sit in her lap, something that had never happened before. She rubbed his back along the spine, and he purred like an ancient but satisfied engine. She was unexpectedly touched by the bare spots on his pelt where he had lost patches of fur to other male cats who were stronger and possibly younger than he.

"You are getting on, aren't you, and spoiled, a huge, enormous, over-indulged cat!" she said to him. "I always thought you were macho itself."

He purred.

"Is it affection you need? Or a handout? You

have your nerve asking me, after doing away with my seven Alphas."

Nevertheless she buttered a piece of toast generously for him and placed her not quite finished omelet on the floor, although had Mrs. Simmons seen Marmaduke licking the plate, there would have been a riot.

The cat, having finished his meal, walked over to the back door and waited patiently for Suzy to open it. Was he getting milder in his dotage? she wondered. She had always thought of him meowing a loud, insistent command as he waited to go out. Suzy opened the door and watched him stroll through the garden.

Spring. March, late March with daffodils and narcissi blooming on upright green stems, swaying mildly in the breeze. The almond tree was leafing out into new, fresh leaves and a late ornamental cherry tree was showing off its pink, girlish beauty. Birds darted back and forth, chirping, singing, scolding, and laying claims to this branch or that in a passion of nest building.

Why should the whole world be so happy when I'm so miserable, Suzy moaned.

She poured another cup of coffee for herself, but could not drink it. Once more she tried the Bradbury but could not see the words for the tears that rose in her eyes, as if she had some dreadful eye disease. At this rate she couldn't possibly face the family.

There was only one thing to do, get dressed and leave.

Chapter 17

Five minutes later, in jeans and a tee shirt with Einstein's formula emblazoned on it (gift of Brother Big Brain), she left the house, unlocked her ten speed, and escaped.

The whole town slept except for an ancient lady, still in a faded negligee, who was happily cutting branches of flowering quince from her garden. She waved at Suzy who waved back. At least this avid gardener most likely did not know Suzy's tragedy.

She rode to the outskirts of the Heights, past a new subdivision in construction, after which fields and orchards rolled pleasantly in the morning sun. It was a landscape Suzy loved, an occasional old farmhouse, a barn leaning and weathered, a grove of eucalyptus, and sometimes a private road leading to a mansion, disguised as a casual cabin, hidden in the redwoods. Three sleek reddish-brown horses grazed in a pasture and a new colt frolicked near his mother and then stopped to stare at Suzy. For at least a few minutes she forgot Peter while she admired the colt.

And yet she was miserable, so miserable she would not be able to tell anyone of her suffering. No, she must not tell anyone, not even Mousie and Patty.

The road became hilly, and then flattened out. She realized with something of a surprise that without planning to do so, she had nearly reached San Julio where the Animal Shelter was located. Until she worked on *Oklahoma*, she had visited the shelter several times a month and had talked with all the animals, since she was sure they were lonesome, and had exercised many of them in the large exercise yard. How many times had she held these unwanted cats and dogs close to her, wishing she could take them all home with her or at least free them from their cages.

Would the shelter be open early on a Sunday morning? She turned off at the narrow side road that led to the brown clapboard building where the sounds of cats crying and dogs barking and whimpering filled her with sadness, guilt, and an inextinguishable love.

Mr. Morales, the caretaker, a short, heavyset man, was hosing down the cages, but the foul odor of imprisoned animals persisted.

" 'allo, Suzy, you here again? I mees you. Where you been all thees time? I used to think maybe you want to live here."

"I wish I could. I've been busy, but now I'll be coming back."

"Sure, you good girl. The dogs, they love you. Hey, whassamatter? You look sad. Something happen, Suzy?"

Immediately Suzy brightened, forcing a wide smile. "Everything's fine."

"Jus' the same, I theenk maybe today you take home with you a nice sweet kitty or a cute puppy. My, do we have sweet little doggies! You could use a nice l'il frien'. You want one real bad, huh?"

"Yes. I've always wanted one." The tears were threatening again.

"So why don' you find yourself a puppy? I got a beauty, jus' right for you."

"I can't. You know that. They won't let me have one."

"But why? If you want a dog, you should have one."

"We've got this cat. He's big and tough."

"Ah, you're afraid the dog will hurt the cat?"

"No, the other way around. That cat is a killer. He could kill a dog. Really he could."

Mr. Morales laughed and scratched his head. "I seen cats like that too. I don' get close; they could chew your arm off."

"Actually, I'm not so sure that Marmaduke is that mean," Suzy said hesitantly. After all, he had been very pleasant that morning. "Mr. Morales, could I say hello to the cats and dogs, and maybe exercise some?"

"Sure. Suzy, I have some work to do, but you go ahead and see if you can find that nice little dog I theenk is just right for you."

She smiled. "I'll bet I can find him."

She sobered as she walked through the cat section. The younger kittens clawed at the wires and mewed at her in high voices, like orphans in old fashioned stories, each crying "Take me, take me!"

"I would if I could, you darlings," she said.

The older cats neither mewed nor tried to get her attention, but folded their paws under them and closed their eyes into narrow slits. Nobody would want to rescue them. They knew this. Too old, too battle scarred, too covered with fleas. They had given up hope, knowing that death waited for them. The old ones did not eat the food that Mr. Morales placed in the cages each day, as if there were no point in it or they preferred to starve to death.

Would Suzy send Marmaduke here? Never. Never. No matter how many parakeets he had murdered and how many other crimes he had committed, (that is, her parents thought of them as crimes), she would not allow him to be put in jail here.

The dogs were placed on the other side of the shelter. Suzy stopped to watch a cage of puppies, some of them very young roly polys wrestling with one another playfully as if there were nothing the least bit morbid about their circumstance. Others either slept or were too weak to get up, but a number of them scrambled to the front of the cage to greet Suzy. In spite of all her troubles, she had to smile at them and call them sweet, foolish names.

Further on, larger dogs paced up and down in their cages. How could anyone not want them, she wondered, for many were beautiful animals, possibly pure-bred. Still others, though cross-bred, were obviously intelligent, splendid animals. It was tragic that they should be so imprisoned, and that if not adopted, they would be put to death. As their brown beseeching eyes met Suzy's she longed to fling open the doors and let them free.

"Watch out for thees one," Mr. Morales warned

as he came up behind Suzy. "Thees German shepherd, something happen, he can be mean. But thees other one here, thees aristocrat, ah, what a dog! An Afghan. You know the breed, h'm?"

The Afghan reminded her of Peter as he stood his ground proudly. Handsome, swift, princely. . . was that the dog Mr. Morales had chosen for her?

She went on, pausing at each cage, saying hello to each animal, and yet she had not found one that would seem to belong to her until she reached the next to the last cage. There a young dog, not a puppy and yet not mature, stood on his hind legs as Suzy approached, wagged his tail with pleasure and seemed to ask Suzy to play with him. She could not make out his parentage. Probably a mix of terrier, poodle, and something else, though it hardly mattered. Some ancestor had given him a coat of thick, curly, brown fur with white paws and a mischievous white forelock. Immediately Suzy knew this would be her dog.

"Hello there! What's your name? Do you want to come home with me?"

An affirmative wag of the tail.

"So you found heem, Suzy? That's the one, exactly right for you. Yesterday a nice lady bring him in. Two kids crying to beat the band, but the landlord won't allow animals. His name is Boots, 'cause of the white fur on his paws. A good name, no?"

"He's perfect, Mr. Morales. If only I could take him. But I have to ask my mother and father."

"Thees story I hear all the time. You think they say yes?"

"No, because of the cat," she sighed. "How much time does Boots have before. . .you know. . .if someone doesn't adopt him?"

136

"It depends. We get lots of new puppies in the spring, the older dogs have to go to make room." Mr. Morales lifted his shoulders helplessly.

"Mr. Morales, could you keep him for me, please?"

"If I can. But Suzy, if someone else wants him, I can't say no."

Slowly she nodded her head in agreement.

"Well, could I exercise him a little?"

"Of course." Mr. Morales gave her a leash, opened the door of the cage, and Boots jumped on Suzy, yipping happily, tail wagging and ears alert. She hugged Boots, feeling the warm sturdy body and admiring the rakish lock of hair that accented his brown forehead. Yes, this must be her dog!

She took him out to the exercise yard and ran with him, then picked up a ball and played with him, and even taught him to sit on command, when Mr. Morales called out that somebody was there to see him and it was time to put Boots back in his cage. Ruefully, Suzy brought Boots back indoors, but before she left the shelter she whispered in his ear, "Wait for me, Boots, I'll be back to get you."

All the way home she had to think of how to get hold of Boots. If only Marmaduke could be encouraged to run under the wheel of an approaching car or fall in a swimming pool. On second thought, she took it all back. She wouldn't want to see him suffer and could not even wish death for him. Was it possible to encourage him to run away of his own accord?

She was nearly home when she realized that in the last hour and a half or so, she had been able to forget Peter and the dance. She had been quite herself once more and what a relief that had been! Maybe that was the way to cure herself!

"Well, here she is at last! Where've you been? And how was the dance? You'll have to tell us about it. We're dying to know," Mrs. Simmons said as she poured blueberry pancake batter in the sizzling pan.

"Can I have some pancakes? I'm starving," Suzy said. "The dance was okay."

"Only 'okay'? What about Peter?" Cynthia asked. "He is SO CUTE. Is he gonna take you out again?"

"He's very nice but I don't think I'll go out with him again," Suzy said coolly, not a trace of a tear, not a giveaway tone in her voice. "Mom, isn't there any yogurt?"

"Suzy, you haven't told us what the dance was like. Did you dance with anyone beside Peter? Did everyone like your dress?" Mrs. Simmons asked.

"For heaven's sake. I told you, it was all right. Nice. A dance, that's all. I danced a lot with Peter and the captain of the football team asked me if I wanted to dance..."

"And what did you say?" Cynthia cried, her eyes open wide.

"I told him no," Suzy said, which may possibly have given her some status in her sister's eyes. "Listen, Mom, this morning I went to the shelter and I saw the most remarkable dog. You'd love him..."

"Suzy, are you starting up that dog business again?" Mrs. Simmons sighed. "You know we just can't take a chance with Marmaduke."

"I'm not so sure that Marmaduke wants to fight all that much."

"Wanna bet on it?" Cynthia asked.

"Here, take this pancake, dear. It's perfect! Sorry about the dog," Mrs. Simmons said.

"You could try! Mom, I don't think you even listen to me! Marmaduke is changing."

"Cats don't change. Now, I don't want to hear another word about it. There, don't let your pancake get cold."

"Don't want it," Suzy said, pushing her plate away. "Welcome to the real world!"

Without another word she went up to her room. Fortunately she remembered that the next day would bring a comprehensive, important math test to see who would get into the advanced program. With relief, she plunged into an intense review which succeeded temporarily in shutting out thoughts of Peter, the dance, and even Boots.

Chapter 18

Dreaded Mondays cannot be kept away. It came and Suzy hid under the covers. Should she pretend a cold and stay home? She considered it, then remembered the math test, and so sprang out of bed. She couldn't possibly allow Daniel Bright to get ahead of her.

She would play it cool, pretend indifference. By this time her tear ducts were reasonably emptied and her eyes dry, but of course there was no saying what would happen should she see Peter again, and most likely she would pass him in the hall. She had been in love and now it was all over, but she still ached.

That was bad enough, but the fear of being stared at, laughed at, known as the girl that Peter ditched at the dance. . .that would be too much.

Courage! She had no choice but to face it and get it over with.

Patty and Mousie, calling for her early, were bursting with questions.

"Why didn't you call us yesterday and tell us about it? What was he like? How late did you stay out? Did you dance every dance? Did he kiss you? How did you get to the dance?"

Suzy curled her lips in what she hoped was a mysterious smile, an "I'm-not-telling" kind of smile.

"I can't answer everything. Really! We went in a cute, antique MG. Loved it. We danced a lot and Peter's very nice. As for kissing. . .I don't exactly kiss and tell, not me." She hoped they would interpret this as something more than a perfunctory peck on the cheek.

"Oh wow," Patty said. "You've got all the luck."

"Have I?"

"Is he really in love with you? Is he going to take you out?" Mousie asked.

Suzy wanted to say calmly, "No, we won't be going out again because he's really in love with Melissa," but her voice began to choke, so she shrugged her shoulders. Before the morning was over, they'd find out the truth. When it was really over and she had healed, she would be able to talk about her broken heart.

The attitude should be one of pride, possibly indifference. Never had her posture been better, stiff perhaps, but definitely straight. Suzy walked into the school and down the hall waiting for rude remarks, knowing smiles, and barbed comments. What happened? Nothing. Nobody seemed to notice her.

Peter, walking down the hall with his hand on the back of Melissa's neck, exactly as it was before the feud began, saw her.

"Hi, Suzy!" he smiled, nodding pleasantly and walking on.

"Hello, Peter," she said coolly, casually, as though they had always known each other. Casual friends. Her heart was breaking at the sight of him, but the tears stayed back in place. A victory.

A few boys said hello to Suzy. Freshmen. No malice that she could detect, so she smiled back easily enough with a friendly "Hi."

"How was it?" Terry asked in the locker room. "I looked for you but couldn't find you."

"It was crowded, for sure. Did you have a good time?" Suzy asked.

"Sure. But how was Peter? Did he behave?"

"But you were there, Terry. Didn't you see him making up with Melissa?" There, it was out. She had said it first, which made it easier to face.

"We thought that would happen. Peter's like that. I guess we should have warned you about that."

"It's all right," Suzy said, then grew trusting. "Mostly I was afraid everybody would laugh at me. I mean, it was embarrassing."

"Don't give it a second thought. It happens all the time," Billie said. "It happens to other people too, not just Peter."

"Anyway," Terry added, "getting Peter to take you to the Spring Dance is something to be proud about. If you only knew how many girls were jealous of you."

"Jealous? Of me? Maybe Melissa, but not me," Suzy said.

Maybe what they said was actually true or they were simply making it easier for her. Still she fretted. But nothing happened. No sneers, no mean remarks, and best of all, no sympathetic glances from those who knew about what had happened.

So I'm Suzy Nobody again, she said to herself. How could a thought be comforting and disturbing at the same time?

In math class she found another note on her desk in a hastily devised envelope. The same neat writing as last time.

"You're okay. Don't take it so hard," it said.

Well, really, what nerve! she thought. Someone had seen through her proud posture and pretended reserve. Still it was reassuring to be told she was all right.

Then the math test was given out. Everything else disappeared, Peter, Melissa, Marmaduke, Boots, and the rivalry between Suzy Somebody, Suzy Nobody and Suzy, Plain Suzy. The universe shrank to the paper on the desk before her and stayed that way for fifty minutes until the bell released her.

Chapter 19

Many books had been written about falling in love, but few about falling out of love, which was not so easy as it might seem at first. Getting over Peter was like working out of a bad habit or a secret vice. For months now, a kind of daydream, an endless moving picture featuring herself and Peter had been playing in her head. In spite of herself, it persisted.

Even four days after the Spring Dance, as she scraped the dinner dishes and put them in the dishwater, she found herself embroidering another Peter-Suzy story. This time several years had passed. Now a rising young mathematician, she was attending a crucial conference in Paris when, walking along the Seine, she bumps into a tall, blond man. Suzy! Peter! They embrace warmly, sit at a sidewalk cafe and catch up with what has happened. Melissa has long departed, having married a fat beer-drinking slob and mothered five dreadful children. Peter is acting in the Paris theater but he is lonely, very lonely. Now he sees Suzy in another light. I'm falling in love, he confesses. . ."

Cut!

Enough garbage, she told herself sternly. From now on she would not permit the slightest image of Peter. Before she even finished the dishes she rushed upstairs and took down all the newspaper pictures of Peter as well as a fading proof of a more formal photograph that she had picked up from a wastebasket. At first she was tempted to throw them away, hesitated, then filed them in back of a stout and ancient volume on the History of Dentistry that her father once gave her.

Satisfied with her strength of character, Suzy returned to the kitchen. What would she think of then?

Anything. She made up a problem. If a room measured 15 feet and two inches in length, $13\frac{2}{3}$ feet in width, and $23\frac{1}{4}$ feet in height, quick, what was its cubic volume? Quick, quick, quick, Ms. Simmons!

Falling out of love did not happen all at once. For four days she walked around with what she believed to be an aching heart. It surprised her to find this was not merely a figure of speech. Though she knew her heart was as healthy as a heart could be, still it ached dully. She was all too aware of an emptiness where the dreams of Peter used to be. Even the excitement of being one of the very few and the only freshman who was admitted to the accelerated math program did not cure the dull pain that followed the end of her first love.

"I'll Never Fall in Love Again!" More than

once she found herself singing this song. An old enough song, but the sentiment held.

On Thursday afternoon, still another neatly written note appeared on her desk. Who was doing this? The mystery was solved this time.

Suzy, there's a sci-fic festival at the Varsity on Friday, 3 flics, two of them terrific and I haven't seen the third. Want to come with me?

d.b.

Suzy looked at him and found Daniel had been watching her read the note. How he blushed! Suzy grinned at him. Three science-fiction films were exactly what she could use at this point. She nodded her head with a vigorous yes. Thanks, I'd love to go, she mouthed.

Strange, strange! So it had been Daniel who had written those other notes to her. But why? And why had he waited so long to ask her? She would find out. All through math class Suzy's mind wandered. Why, Daniel would be a perfect solution, for with him there would be no spinning of fantasies or falling in love. Chances were that the conversation would never go dry.

"If you don't mind," Suzy explained apologetically as they made arrangements after class, "you'll have to meet my parents first. They're fussy, but don't get involved in a conversation with my father, or we'll never get out. Okay? You won't mind too much, will you?"

He appeared on Friday night, in clean jeans and a nondescript shirt. Suzy introduced him swiftly to her parents and then whisked him out the front door before her father could make any well-intentioned but disastrous remarks. Then she and Daniel bicycled to the Varsity.

Seeing films with Daniel was hardly the passive experience it was when Suzy sat beside Patty and Mousie, slouched back in their seats and eating popcorn while the movie rolled. Daniel sat up alertly and in a low voice pointed out every flaw and inconsistency in the film, which annoyed everyone around them except Suzy, who managed to find a few errors as well. She also found out that she and Daniel laughed out loud at whatever they found funny, although the rest of the audience remained sober. However, the obvious jokes which set the crowd roaring frequently left them straight faced and unmoved.

It's amazing, Suzy was thinking, that after fourteen years of life on this planet, I have found someone who thinks the way I do.

"Shall we go to the Good Earth?" Daniel asked as they walked out of the theater, somewhat groggy after three films.

The Good Earth was a health-food, frozen-yogurt, secondhand-paperback place, not as crowded as Fountain Blue nor as noisy, a place where college students tended to gather. Instead of a dance floor, the room was filled with small tables. Several chess games were going on as Daniel and Suzy entered.

They sat in a corner booth and Daniel invited Suzy to join him in his favorite concoction, yogurt mixed with peanut butter and honey, accompanied by Himalayan Seed Cookies.

Had Suzy thought Daniel shy? If so, she would never think so again. Once he began to speak there was no stopping him, although now and then he thrust a question at Suzy and waited to see what she would say, his brown eyes burning behind his glasses. Once or twice they disagreed on such matters as the technicalities involved in science-fiction films, but for the most part they agreed. They began to speak of books they had read and theories they had come across. Daniel ordered a pot of rose hip tea and more Himalayan Seed Cookies and they drank tea and nibbled cookies and could have gone on talking all night until Sam, the owner, came over and leaned on their table.

"If you don't mind my mentioning it," Sam said, "you may have noticed people coming in and going out? Unfortunately, getting up and leaving this haven is part of the scene."

"I'm sorry. I hadn't noticed," Daniel said, becoming shy once more.

"That's all right. To be expected. But it's after midnight and we have to close down before we turn back into mice and pumpkins. So if you don't mind. . ."

"Is it that late? My mother will kill me. My father will be furious," Suzy said, getting up.

Daniel paid the bill and as they left, Sam shouted after them, "Come back again, now!"

"We will!" Daniel promised.

They bicycled home slowly. They did not speak but the silence was comfortable. They passed a eucalyptus grove and discovered they both loved the pungent scent although not everyone found it pleasant. They stopped at an empty lot briefly to gaze up at the stars.

"When I look up at them, I can hardly believe

the distances," Suzy said. "You can learn all the light years, but it's almost impossible to conceive of it. I mean, it's hard to take it all in. And yet I'd love to go up there. Do you ever think about going into space?"

"Sometimes. It takes real heroes, real courage. I'm not sure about going out there exactly, but I'd love to work behind the scenes, maybe at NASA. There's so much I have to learn before I decide anything."

"Me too. Like astronomy. It really turns me on."

"Suzy, have you ever gone to the Planetarium in San Francisco?"

"No, have you? Is it really good?"

"Sometimes it's terrific. Maybe we could get the Science Club to charter a bus to go there."

"I'm not in the Science Club."

"I know, Suzy. You should be. Some people are doing terrific things, experiments, projects."

"I didn't know freshmen could belong. Maybe it's too late," Suzy said, suddenly wanting to be part of it and yet fearful that she wasn't bright enough.

"Special people can belong. And you're special. I wanted to ask you before. . .I wanted to ask you lots of things before. . ."

Daniel stopped gazing at the stars, but glanced at Suzy, then studied the hole in his tennis shoe. Suzy felt him hesitating and growing shy again.

"What kind of things did you want to ask me?" Suzy asked softly. "And why didn't you?"

"I don't know. I'd never asked any girl anything. I used to imagine it would be nice to go bicycle riding together, or play chess, or go to

Science Club, but I was afraid you'd turn me down. And then there was all that business with you and Peter. I mean, you can see an awful lot, even if you're just making stage sets."

"Why did you warn me not to go to the dance with Peter?" Suzy asked, her voice low and trembling. If he spoke, suggesting that he knew it would only end in pain for Suzy, it would not be easy to take. Had he known she was in love with Peter and that it would never work?

"I wrote the note because. . .well, I guess I was jealous, not of Peter, of course, because I never wanted to be a dancing boy, but because you were going with him. In a funny way it gave me the courage to ask you, so I wouldn't lose out altogether."

"Do you mean it?"

"Sure. First you'd go with Peter and even though he went back to Melissa, I thought maybe Sakovich would ask you, and then somebody else. So I just had to get in there first."

Suzy laughed, but did not answer. Anyone would think there was a long line of boys waiting to take her out to hear Daniel talk, but if that was his illusion, she decided to let him keep it.

"I really have to get home," she said.

Once more they bicycled slowly until they reached Suzy's house, and then they stood on the sidewalk and talked some more. It was as if they were friends who had been separated for years and had to catch up on everything.

Suddenly a light blazed in an upstairs window and Dr. Simmons appeared. He thrust his head out of the window.

"Suzy, are you there? Do you know what time

it is? You come up now, this minute. I want to talk with you."

The irritated tone in his voice ended the spell of the evening.

"Do you think I should say good night to your father?" Daniel asked in a loud whisper.

"I think you should just go home," Suzy whispered back. "Thanks a lot, Daniel. I had a good time. Good night."

"See ya," Daniel said, pedaling away while Suzy locked her bike and rushed upstairs to reassure her father that everything was all right.

Chapter 20

It's not easy to drop a great love, Suzy decided. In spite of what seemed to be a growing friendship with Daniel and the flattery of having been especially invited to join the prestigious Science Club, still the sight of Peter striding through the halls or heading for the tennis courts, racquet in hand, still shocked Suzy as though an electric current ran through her. Never again, she moaned to herself, would she ever find anyone as ideal as Peter. Beside him, every male was diminished. And Daniel? Well, that was a different matter. They could not really be compared.

Yet more than any of this was eclipsed by another concern, the image of a small, brown dog with white paws and a mischievous white forelock. It was nearly two weeks since Suzy had visited the shelter and the time was drawing close when Boots might be "put to sleep" if he were not adopted. More and more puppies and stray dogs were being brought to the shelter and room had to be made for them.

How Suzy detested that phrase, "put to sleep"! No matter how humanely it was done, still it meant death, the killing of that loving little creature, stilling him forever.

And Boots was her dog. She felt this instinctively without a doubt. They belonged together.

Marmaduke would live forever. Nine lives? More like ninety. Even though he had become quite affectionate toward Suzy, still this big hulking cat was closer to the jungle than to Elmwood Heights. A battered veteran of many battles, he must have been the victor more than once, for a hundred gingery little kittens in Elmwood Heights resembled him. Marmaduke swaggered through the Simmons' household as though he owned it, committing unspeakable crimes in the indoor garden, bringing in half eaten or still struggling bluejays and robins to breathe their last breath at Mrs. Simmons' feet, and occasionally he threw up on the new oriental rug.

"But I can't get rid of him, in spite of all that," Mrs. Simmons said. "It's Cynthia's cat. You can ruin a child's life by getting rid of a pet. Child psychologists say this all the time."

A hopeless situation, Suzy thought. And yet if her mother offered to take Marmaduke to the shelter, Suzy would have been the first to object. "Mom, you can't just kill an animal!"

And yet that's exactly what would happen to Boots if he weren't adopted. If only Marmaduke would run away. Or drop dead of old age. After all, he was getting on, napping more than previously, Suzy noticed, and wanting to be petted. From time to time he even rubbed against Dr. Simmons' leg. "You're not getting around me!" her father warned.

Early on a Saturday morning, close to that time when Boots' period of grace would come to an end, Cynthia sat watching cartoons on television while Suzy sat glumly over breakfast. All night long she had dreamed of Boots and now she knew she must think of something to save him.

"No solution, no solution," she moaned to herself, when a screech of brakes and the pained yowl of a cat tore through the peaceful quiet of Manzanita Lane, even overpowering the cartoon show. Then silence.

"Marmaduke!"

Suzy rushed into the living room. "Hey, Cynthia, didn't you hear the cat? I think Marmaduke's been run over. Come on, let's see."

"I wanna finish the program first," Cynthia said, her eyes never leaving the screen.

Suzy ran out into the street. Whatever car had struck the cat had disappeared and Marmaduke lay in the middle of the street. Dead? Dying? Marmaduke lay still, his eyes glazed with pain. Yet there was no blood, no immediate sign of his having been crushed by the wheel. Suzy picked him up and held him in her arms.

"Marmaduke, don't die!"

Why, she cared! She really cared. She carried him to the sidewalk and nearly wept over him. In a few minutes he revived, let Suzy stroke him and console him and even gratified her by giving her a low, rusty purr. It amazed her, that Marmaduke could be such a. . .such a *pussycat*! Then he begged to be let down, which Suzy did with gentle care and he walked away, limping badly. Still he turned once to glance gratefully at Suzy.

And then the problem was solved. Suzy saw it immediately although it had been clear all along. Why couldn't Marmaduke get along with a dog, particularly if it were a young vigorous dog like Boots? A year ago, possibly two years ago or three, the idea would be unthinkable. But now Marmaduke was getting to be an old man, a wounded old man. He might choose not to fight a dog.

Suzy ran upstairs to her parents' bedroom and woke her father. "Dad? Marmaduke was nearly run over. He's okay but I think his paw is badly hurt. Can you take him to the vet?"

"Not now, Suzy," her father said sleepily. "No vet in his right mind would be awake at this hour. But I'll take him to Dr. Steiner's on my way to work."

"Terrific!" she said. Poor Dad! Although he had long complained about Marmaduke, he was the one who always took him to the vet's and took care of his licensing and other needs.

Suzy then dressed quickly, took the allowance she had been saving for this very purpose, and peddled off as fast as she could to the Animal Shelter.

One last prayer. "Please, let him be there, waiting for me!"

However, it was early in the morning and she was the one who had to wait on the porch of the shelter until Mr. Morales arrived.

"Hey, Suzy? How long you been here, huh? Am I late? Are you early? You waitin' for that doggie?"

"Yeah. Mr. Morales, is he still there? Is he all right?"

"Sure, but very sad. Nobody wants him. He don' eat nothin'."

"I do, Mr. Morales. I want to take him home with me."

"Let's go ask Boots and see what he says about that. Okay?"

They walked back to where Boots lay, thin and sad. Had he lost his spirit or had he been sleeping? As he saw Suzy approach, his ears pricked up.

"Boots, hello Boots! I'm here!"

At the sound of her voice, he revived, leaped to his feet and wagged his tail so hard it was a miracle it didn't fall off. Mr. Morales opened the door to his cage and Boots jumped into Suzy's arms and let her hold him close as if he would never let go.

"Okay, so he likes you and you like him. But what about that mean old cat at your house, eh?"

"Well, Mr. Morales, he's getting to be an old man. I think we can work things out."

"Your parents, what about them? They say okay?"

"I didn't ask them, 'cause they'd only say no. But it's going to be all right. If they make Boots go, I'll go too."

Mr. Morales' eyes gleamed. "You sure love that doggie. He's got it made. I gotta ask this, Suzy, you want to make contribution for care of the animals?"

"Sure," Suzy said. Money in itself was nothing, but in terms of saving lives it was important. What she had to pay was not much, but she paid it happily. She signed the necessary adoption papers and then asked Mr. Morales if she could borrow a leash, because she was on her bicycle.

"And you will return it, won't you? Sure you will, you're a good girl wit' a good heart."

156

"Thanks, Mr. Morales," she said. It was good to be trusted.

She attached the leash to Boots' collar and rode home slowly on her bicycle. From time to time she stopped to let him rest, for he wasn't used to exercise. Each time she sat beside the road and hugged him while he looked up into her eyes as if to say, "I'm yours now, Suzy. I'm where I belong."

"Terrific, terrific!" she said. For once in her life she had acted on her own. It was no accident that she found herself humming "Oh, What a Beautiful Morning" as she rode home with Boots trotting beside her.

Chapter 21

What makes a person change? The old rating in which Suzy judged everyone somewhere between one and ten no longer seemed to work. People were too complex to be put into numbers and besides, they moved about too much, moving from one category to another. She herself was metamorphosing into a new Suzy and yet if she had to explain just how this was happening, she would not have been able to do so. Nor could she tell exactly when it began, although she suspected it may have started when she joined the Costume Crew or even before that when she first saw Peter and fell in love. But since the dreadful night of the dance, other events were occurring, surprising her so that she scarcely recognized herself.

An example.

One night Daniel called. "Hey, Suzy, I've just come across some neat new puzzles in the *Scientific American*. I'll bet you can't do them."

"I'll bet I can."

"Ho, ho, ho! Can you meet me in the library tonight at 7:30?"

"Right."

Of course Suzy could have invited Daniel to her house, but Mrs. Simmons would insist on making blueberry pancakes for Daniel and asking all kinds of questions about his family, questions that would surely embarrass Suzy; or Dr. Simmons would want some advice on a piece of sculpture he was making; as for Cynthia, she was unbearable. Better to go to the library.

No sooner had Daniel hung up, than the phone rang again.

"Guess who, Suzy!" the voice said.

"Kate! Katie Osborne. Hi! Haven't seen you for a long time."

"It's not my fault. Every time I called, you were working on *Oklahoma* or something. Listen, Suzy, I'm in real trouble. A big math test tomorrow. Only you can help me through it because you're so terrific. If I don't pass it, my parents'll kill me. Can you come over?"

"I'd like to help, but I've got an appointment."

"An *appointment*? You mean you've got a date? Or something serious? Look, Suzy, if it weren't *important*, I wouldn't *ask* you, but my father'll throttle me if I don't come through."

"Is it really that bad?"

"It's gonna be a killer. Please, Suzy, you can tell your guy you'll see him another time. This is important. If you don't come, I'll cut my throat or something."

How violent she sounds, Suzy was thinking. What

159

kind of person was Kate anyway? In the past she had only thought of her as someone who had friends but now she wondered if Kate was really her friend.

"Suzy? Are you there?" Kate's voice changed, becoming friendlier. "Did you know I'm going to have a really big party in May? Of course you're invited. Only if I don't pass the test tomorrow, there won't be any party."

Suzy frowned. This was the old Kate, making promises which she never kept, yet Suzy kept helping her in the hope that maybe she would invite her to one of her popular parties. Now Suzy would no longer be fooled.

"Kate," she said in a voice so calm and positive, she hardly recognized it as her own. "You can do that math by yourself. You don't need me. All you have to do is concentrate."

"But I caaaaan't, Suzy. Suzy, please. . ." Kate appeared to be on the edge of tears, but Suzy would not budge. To help was one thing; to be used another.

"You can do it, Kate. Tell yourself that you can. Then sit in a quiet place. Take it slowly, one step at a time. It's all logical. It makes sense. It's not hard if you go at it right."

"You're mean, Suzy Simmons," Kate said. "You never used to be like this. Just because you went out with Peter Gilbert, you think you're something. Well, you're not! Not by a long shot!" Kate said, slamming down the receiver.

"Of course I'm something! At least she thinks so," Suzy said to herself as she put down the receiver. She smiled and then she began to laugh. It was so simple, she thought, not letting herself be bullied any more. All she had to say was no when it seemed the right thing to do. Why had it taken her so long to learn to do it? As for that party in May, she didn't need it, not one bit.

As she combed her hair, which was definitely getting longer, she grinned at herself in the mirror. She was beginning to like herself, a strange new experience.

Chapter 22

One morning in May Suzy was out jogging with Boots running along beside her, when she saw another jogger, all in white, coming in her direction. Peter! Peter on this crisp early morning when the sun was shining through the new green leaves of the trees above and the air was still cool and fresh with the scent of roses. It could have been a romantic idyll.

"Hi, Suzy!" he called out and slowed down a little, as if he might have consented to talk with her.

"Hi, Peter!" she said and kept on running. It was only five minutes later that it occurred to her that she no longer felt a thumping of the heart when she saw him. Any thumping was purely the result of jogging. She supposed she could have stopped and talked with him, and yet she didn't.

She breathed freely and deeply. The tragedy was over!

After lunch, Suzy was washing Boots in the back yard. He was drying himself in a time-honored dog tradition of shaking and soaking everyone around him, including Marmaduke who hissed and walked on in affronted dignity. It was then that Suzy noticed her mother stood at the door and watched the spectacle.

"Suzy, I think it's time we had a little talk. Will you come in?"

"You mean one of those mother-daughter things? We had that in gym. You don't have to tell me."

"That's not what I meant, but something else, just as important," Mrs. Simmons said. "I'll be on the patio."

Suzy suspected her mother's confidential chats, but appeared anyway. She sat on one of the wrought-iron chairs, barely missing the caress of a trailing fern that hung from one of the many pots around the patio.

"Can I get you something?" Mrs. Simmons asked. "A frozen yogurt? Iced tea? Glass of milk?"

"Mom, I just had lunch. Remember? What do you want to talk about?"

"Don't sound so hostile. I want to talk about you. This has been a year of great change for you. Your father and I are pleased."

Suzy should have said thank you, but instead she grunted.

"You've gone to an important dance. You took part in a play production. You got into the Advanced Math program. You made the Science Club. And you have a nice friend. Daniel is a little strange, not what I would have chosen, but very nice. Bright."

"Yeah, Mom. Daniel Bright! Ha ha!"

Her mother sighed but held her temper. Suzy

was wiggling her toes and from time to time staring pointedly at her watch, but Mrs. Simmons kept on.

"All I want to say is that it's time you found new friends. You've been seeing Mousie and Patty every day now for years. Now they may be very nice girls, but they are both immature. To be frank about it, they are drags. Neither of them are very attractive, not particularly bright. You know the old saying, birds of a feather flock together. It means you get to be like the people you go with. Would you really want to be like Mousie or Patty?"

Suzy stirred uncomfortably. The same thought had been on her mind since the beginning of the school year. Yet she found herself defending them.

"They're my friends, Mom. Real friends. You just don't throw that away."

"I agree. Friendship is sacred. But are you sure they're your friends? You see, they use you. Patty is always trying to get you to eat all those sweet starchy foods she makes. She was on the telephone this morning asking you to come over and try some eclairs she'd just baked. As for Mousie, she's forever crying on your shoulder. By the way, she called too."

"Why didn't you tell me?" Suzy cried, standing up. "They'll be hurt if I don't call them back."

"I just told you, didn't I?" Mrs. Simmons answered. "Don't misunderstand, Suzy. Friendship is fine, but it's important to make friends with lively, stimulating people, not those girls who will drag you down with them."

Suzy flushed. She had thought exactly what her mother was now saying. Yet hearing it out loud made her feel ashamed.

"If they can drag me down with them, maybe I can pull them up. Right?" Suzy asked.

"It's almost impossible. But I wish you'd think about it. Would you do that?"

Mrs. Simmons was not exactly unreasonable.

"Okay," Suzy promised. "I will."

"That's my girl," Mrs. Simmons said as she got up to leave, but if she saw the way her daughter frowned and her lower lip protruded in thought, she would have realized she hadn't won a victory, not yet.

In a way her mother was right, Suzy argued. Still, you don't throw away friends. Besides, she liked a certain warm kitcheny coziness about Patty and even if Mousie complained far too much, still she wrote fascinating murder stories and Suzy was sure she would one day be famous.

Yet they had become somewhat boring. Sometimes she felt herself growing impatient, wanting to shake Patty's shoulders and say, "Hey, you're FAT!" or clapping her hand over Mousie's mouth when she began still another long, tedious complaint. Yet one did not do that. Besides they had been kind to her. If only she could help them. Perhaps if she were to move slowly and carefully. . .

She telephoned Patty first. "Did you call? I was out with Boots."

"Yeah, Suzy. I made some eclairs today. They're yummy. C'mon over and try them."

"Ooh, I'll bet they're good. But I can't, Patty. I'm on a diet."

"You on a diet? But you're so thin."

"Not at all. I have to lose five pounds."

"Who said so?"

"I do. Listen, Patty, I have to exercise Boots. Want to take a walk? Just the two of us?"

Patty sounded surprised. "Just us? Sure. Will you call for me?"

This was something simple and yet they had never done it before, the two of them walking out toward the country while Boots trotted beside them. Without Mousie there to throw cold water on everything Patty had to say, slowly Patty opened up. Suzy knew enough to be a good listener.

"Shall we climb to the top of the hill?"

Patty puffed but climbed, and then they sat under a grove of pines. Shy at first, then bolder as she saw that Suzy understood, Patty spilled out those fears that upset her. "Like I'm not as good as anyone else. Like I'm not really anybody, anybody that matters. Sometimes I think nobody will ever ask me out, not ever."

Suzy nodded. "I know. I used to be just like that. But it doesn't have to be that way. Sometimes it only takes a little thing to change the whole way you think. It has to start inside of you."

"If only I weren't so fat — " Patty began to say, then her sentence drifted off. She had never mentioned before that she knew.

The afternoon sun began to sink and they got up and walked home. Somehow something had happened. Patty decided to go on a diet, but Suzy had somehow agreed to keep her company.

"Oh, dear," she said at dinner when her mother brought in a triumph of a strawberry shortcake. She allowed herself two strawberries without biscuits, without sugar, without whipped cream. Good heavens, what had she done? No more yogurt with honey and peanut butter! No more blueberry pancakes on a Sunday morning!

How Suzy hated diets, but if it would help Patty, then it was all right.

Mousie's case would be more complicated. That evening Suzy phoned and her mother answered.

"Hello, may I please speak to Mary Lou?" Suzy said.

"Mary Lou? You mean Mousie. Of course."

Mousie answered with a timid hello. A timid voice.

"Hi, Mary Lou. Suzy here."

"What's all the Mary Lou stuff?"

"Don't you like the sound of it? I think it's great. Mary Lou Morgan."

"What's with you, Suzy? Actually, I'm not that crazy about it."

"Mousie Morgan? Is that better?"

"Yech! Let's begin all over again."

"We can't," Suzy said. "We're already here. Anyway, I think Mary Lou Morgan sounds elegant. It's up to you," Suzy said, wondering if she was being officious. "Anyway, I have something to tell you. Kind of a secret in a way. Don't ask me how I know because I can't reveal the sources. But there's going to be a great opening on the school paper next year."

"And what's that got to do with me?"

"If you get in there now and show that you're good at all, you'll have a good chance of getting in on it next year."

"Me? You mean me? On the school paper? That's only for juniors and seniors."

"Who said so? They really need people who

can write. They can always stretch the rules a
little."

"But I don't know if I could do it. I don't know
how."

"You've got to try. They'll help you."

"Well, I don't know."

"What don't you know? This is a good way to
get around."

"Well, maybe I will and maybe I won't."

"Up to you. I've got to go now, do the dishes
and stuff."

"Hey, Suzy. Thanks for telling me. I'll think
about it."

Just possibly, Suzy was thinking, there was a
note of enthusiasm in Mousie's — or possibly Mary
Lou's — voice. And that was all she could do for
her friends that day. The rest would be up to them.

Chapter 23

One June day the Science Club went to Golden Gate Park in San Francisco to visit the science museum, the Steinhart Aquarium, and the Morrison Planetarium where they saw a sky show and heard a lecture about the dimensions of the universe. At three-thirty the show was over and the audience walked out into the sunlit afternoon.

Daniel and Suzy walked with the other members of the club, but then wandered off to sit under a sycamore tree. For a few moments neither of them spoke. The view of the universe they had just had and in particular a discussion about black holes which arose after the formal lecture left them both quiet, possibly shocked.

"It's not that we didn't know about such things before, the distances, the vastness and all that, but seeing it like that is too much," Suzy said.

"Overwhelming," Daniel agreed. "It makes you feel so insignificant, too small to be microscopic."

At that moment a band in the bandshell was tuning up.

"A speck of dust. Nothing much. Nobody," Suzy mused. "Nobody. I used to think of a poem about that. What to hear it?"

Without waiting for an answer, she quoted it.

> I'm nobody! Who are you?
> Are you nobody, too?
> Then there's a pair of us — don't tell!
> They'd banish us, you know.
>
> How dreary to be somebody!
> How public, like a frog
> To tell your name the livelong day
> To an admiring bog!

No sooner had she finished quoting the small and poignant verse of Emily Dickinson, when the band burst into a rock version of "Stars and Stripes Forever," so loud that conversation was impossible. Daniel pulled out an alfalfa sprout and cheese pumpernickel sandwich, left over from lunch, offered to share it with Suzy and when she smiled her regrets, chewed on it solemnly and thoughtfully.

It was a long time since Suzy thought of herself as Suzy Nobody, almost at the beginning of the school year when she had wished for everything like a greedy child. Some of the things she had wished had come true. She had fallen in love and almost regretted the pain of it. She had asked to be invited to a dance, and so that had happened, but with a vengeance. No parties, but possibly, she was thinking, she would give one herself. As for friends, Patty and Mary Lou (who had decided to drop the Mousie nickname) were still there, and Daniel was a good friend. She liked almost everyone in the Science Club. Everything was all right.

Still, who was she? For a while she thought she was Suzy Somebody but that was false, shining by Peter's reflected light. Then she was Suzy-Less-Than-Nobody. And now?

The music stopped and Daniel continued their interrupted conversation. "About that business of being nobody. 'I'm nobody.' Well, I wouldn't say that because I am somebody. Maybe not a great somebody, not a famous somebody, but then I'm not a frog either."

"Peter and Melissa are natural frogs," Suzy said, "in terms of the poem, but that's okay because that's how they're made. If I compare myself to them, I'm nobody. At least I used to feel that way. Nobody."

"You, Suzy? You're very much somebody to me, a lot more than Peter and Melissa could ever be. Maybe it's all relative. If you mean something to somebody, then you are somebody."

"I'd put it a little differently," Suzy said. "If you go on thinking you're nobody, then maybe that's what you become. But if you think of yourself, one tiny speck of dust in the universe that is alive, then you are somebody. That doesn't mean you're the Important Famous Somebody like Peter or Melissa, which is what everyone thinks of first when they say, Oh, so-and-so is really SOMEBODY! But if you think that there you are, maybe small but alive, and at any rate somebody who is unique and not exactly like anyone else, then you are a somebody, even if it's spelled with a small 's.'"

She plucked a round, white michaelmas daisy from the grass and looked into its round, shining face. At that moment everything was clear. Who was

Suzy Who? Suzy What's-her-name? Not Suzy No-body or Suzy Somebody, but just Suzy, sitting there on the grass with Daniel beside her, frowning at his alfalfa sprout sandwich, while the band played and the air was filled with music. Blue skies and puffy clouds above. And on the grass a saucy blue-jay demanding that Daniel give him his sandwich.

The band gave up its attempts at rock to slide into a jazzy version of a medley of old-fashioned waltzes.

"I could stay here all day," Suzy said to Daniel.

"It's heaven," Daniel said, "only I can't decide, is the band out of tune or is that the school bus horn?"

The other members of the Science Club were getting up and strolling over to the bus, and the President of the club was rounding up members, but missed Suzy and Daniel.

"Let's wait just two minutes more," Suzy begged. "They won't go without us, and I want to hear the music."

And so they waited. After a while the waltz medley was ended and above the applause the horn of the bus honked impatiently. Suzy and Daniel got up and raced across the grass toward the waiting bus.